EVERYMAN, I will go with thee,

and be thy guide,

In thy most need to go by thy side

DYLAN THOMAS

Born at Swansea, 22 October 1914. Died in New York, 9 November 1953. Buried at Laugharne, Wales.

A PROSPECT
OF THE SEA

and other stories
and prose writings
by
DYLAN THOMAS

Edited by
DANIEL JONES

DENT: LONDON, MELBOURNE AND TORONTO
EVERYMAN'S LIBRARY

*Printed in Great Britain
by Biddles Ltd,
Guildford, Surrey
for
J. M. Dent & Sons Ltd
Aldine House, Welbeck Street, London*

*First published 1955
Aldine paperback edition 1968
Reprinted 1972, 1975
Last reprinted, in Everyman's Library, 1979*

No. 13   Hardback ISBN 0 460 00013 6
No. 1013   Paperback ISBN 0 460 01013 1

PUBLISHER'S NOTE

THE material collected in this volume, which has been edited and arranged by Daniel Jones, was chosen by the author before his death in order to represent, in conjunction with the *Portrait of the Artist as a Young Dog*, such stories and essays as he wished to be preserved.

The source of each item is indicated in the list of contents, and the work has not previously been published in book form in this country with the exception of the stories from *The Map of Love* [1] (now out of print).

[1] The poems from this volume were incorporated in *Collected Poems* during the author's lifetime.

CONTENTS

PART I

A Prospect of the Sea

It was high summer, and the boy was lying in the corn. He was happy because he had no work to do and the weather was hot. He heard the corn sway from side to side above him, and the noise of the birds who whistled from the branches of the trees that hid the house. Lying flat on his back, he stared up into the unbrokenly blue sky falling over the edge of the corn. The wind, after the warm rain before noon, smelt of rabbits and cattle. He stretched himself like a cat, and put his arms behind his head. Now he was riding on the sea, swimming through the golden corn waves, gliding along the heavens like a bird; in seven-league boots he was springing over the fields; he was building a nest in the sixth of the seven trees that waved their hands from a bright, green hill. Now he was a boy with tousled hair, rising lazily to his feet, wandering out of the corn to the strip of river by the hillside. He put his fingers in the water, making a mock sea-wave to roll the stones over and shake the weeds; his fingers stood up like ten tower pillars in the magnifying water, and a fish with a wise head and a lashing tail swam in and out of the tower gates. He made up a story as the fish swam through the gates into the pebbles and the moving bed. There was a drowned princess from a Christmas book, with her shoulders broken and her two red pigtails stretched like the strings of a fiddle over her broken throat; she was caught in a fisherman's net, and the fish plucked her hair. He forgot how the story ended, if ever there were an end to a story that had no beginning. Did the princess live again, rising like

3

a mermaid from the net, or did a prince from another story tauten the tails of her hair and bend her shoulder-bone into a harp and pluck the dead, black tunes for ever in the courts of the royal country? The boy sent a stone skidding over the green water. He saw a rabbit scuttle, and threw a stone at its tail. A fish leaped at the gnats, and a lark darted out of the green earth. This was the best summer since the first seasons of the world. He did not believe in God, but God had made this summer full of blue winds and heat and pigeons in the house wood. There were no chimneys on the hills with no name in the distance, only the trees which stood like women and men enjoying the sun; there were no cranes or coal-tips, only the nameless distance and the hill with seven trees. He could think of no words to say how wonderful the summer was, or the noise of the wood-pigeons, or the lazy corn blowing in the half wind from the sea at the river's end. There were no words for the sky and the sun and the summer country: the birds were nice, and the corn was nice.

He crossed the nice field and climbed the hill. Under the innocent green of the trees, as blackbirds flew out towards the sun, the story of the princess died. That afternoon there was no drowning sea to pull her pigtails; the sea had flowed and vanished, leaving a hill, a cornfield, and a hidden house; tall as the first short tree, she clambered down from the seventh, and stood in front of him in a torn cotton frock. Her bare brown legs were scratched all over, there were berry stains round her mouth, her nails were black and broken, and her toes poked through her rubber shoes. She stood on a hill no bigger than a house, but the field below and the shining strip of river were as little as though the hill were a mountain rising over a single blade and a drop of water; the trees round the farmhouse were firesticks; and the Jarvis peaks, and Cader peak beyond them

to the edge of England, were molehills and stones' shadows
in the still, single yard of the distance. From the first
shade, the boy stared down at the river disappearing, the
corn blowing back into the soil, the hundred house trees
dwindling to a stalk, and the four corners of the yellow field
meeting in a square that he could cover with his hand. He
saw the many-coloured county shrink like a coat in the
wash. Then a new wind sprang from the pennyworth of
water at the river-drop's end, blowing the hill field to its
full size, and the corn stood up as before, and the one stalk
that hid the house was split into a hundred trees. It happened in half a second.

Blackbirds again flew out from the topmost boughs in a
cloud like a cone; there was no end to the black, triangular
flight of birds towards the sun; from hill to sun the winged
bridge mounted silently; and then again a wind blew up, and
this time from the vast and proper sea, and snapped the
bridge's back. Like partridges the common birds fell
down in a shower.

All of it happened in half a second. The girl in the torn
cotton frock sat down on the grass and crossed her legs; a
real wind from nowhere lifted her frock, and up to her
waist she was brown as an acorn. The boy, still standing
timidly in the first shade, saw the broken, holiday princess
die for the second time, and a country girl take her place on
the live hill. Who had been frightened of a few birds
flying out of the trees, and a sudden daze of the sun that
made river and field and distance look so little under the
hill? Who had told him the girl was as tall as a tree?
She was no taller or stranger than the flowery girls on
Sundays who picnicked in Whippet valley.

'What were you doing up the tree?' he asked her,
ashamed of his silence in front of her smiling, and suddenly
shy as she moved so that the grass beneath her rose bent and

green between her brown legs. 'Were you after nests?'
he said, and sat down beside her.   But on the bent grass in
the seventh shade, his first terror of her sprang up again like
a sun returning from the sea that sank it, and burned his
eyes to the skull and raised his hair.   The stain on her lips
was blood, not berries; and her nails were not broken but
sharpened sideways, ten black scissor-blades ready to snip
off his tongue.   If he cried aloud to his uncle in the hidden
house, she would make new animals, beckon Carmarthen
tigers out of the mile-away wood to jump around him and
bite his hands; she would make new, noisy birds in the air
to whistle and chatter away his cries.   He sat very still by
her left side, and heard the heart in her breast drown every
summer sound; every leaf of the tree that shaded them grew
to man-size then, the ribs of the bark were channels and
rivers wide as a great ship; and the moss on the tree, and the
sharp grass ring round the base, were all the velvet coverings
of green county's meadows blown hedge to hedge.   Now on
the world-sized hill, with the trees like heavens holding up
the weathers, in the magnified summer weather she leaned
towards him so that he could not see the cornfield nor his
uncle's house for her thick, red hair; and sky and far ridge
were points of light in the pupils of her eyes.

This is death, said the boy to himself, consumption and
whooping-cough and the stones inside you . . . and the way
your face stays if you make too many faces in the looking-
glass.   Her mouth was an inch from his.   Her long fore-
fingers touched his eyelids.   This is a story, he said to
himself, about a boy on a holiday kissed by a broom-rider;
she flew from a tree on to a hill that changes its size like a
frog that loses its temper; she stroked his eyes and put her
chest against him; and when she had loved him until he died
she carried him off inside her to a den in a wood.   But the
story, like all stories, was killed as she kissed him; now he

was a boy in a girl's arms, and the hill stood above a true river, and the peaks and their trees towards England were as Jarvis had known them when he walked there with his lovers and horses for half a century, a century ago.

Who had been frightened of a wind out of the light swelling the small country? The piece of a wind in the sun was like the wind in an empty house; it made the corners mountains and crowded the attics with shadows who broke through the roof; through the country corridors it raced in a hundred voices, each voice larger than the last, until the last voice tumbled down and the house was full of whispers.

'Where do you come from?' she whispered in his ear. She took her arms away but still sat close, one knee between his legs, one hand on his hands. Who had been frightened of a sunburned girl no taller or stranger than the pale girls at home who had babies before they were married?

'I come from Amman valley,' said the boy.

'I have a sister in Egypt,' she said, 'who lives in a pyramid. . . .' She drew him closer.

'They're calling me in for tea,' he said.

She lifted her frock to her waist.

If she loves me until I die, said the boy to himself under the seventh tree on the hill that was never the same for three minutes, she will carry me away inside her, run with me rattling inside her to a den in a wood, to a hole in a tree where my uncle will never find me. This is the story of a boy being stolen. She has put a knife in my belly and turned my stomach round.

She whispered in his ear: 'I'll have a baby on every hill; what's your name, Amman?'

The afternoon was dying; lazily, namelessly drifting westward through the insects in the shade; over hill and tree and river and corn and grass to the evening shaping in the sea; blowing away; being blown from Wales in a wind, in the slow, blue grains, like a wind full of dreams and medicines; down the tide of the sun on to the grey and chanting shore where the birds from Noah's ark glide by with bushes in their mouths, and to-morrow and to-morrow tower over the cracked sand-castles.

So she stroked her clothes into place and patted back her hair as the day began to die, she rolled over on to her left side, careless of the low sun and the darkening miles.   The boy awoke cautiously into a more curious dream, a summer vision broader than the one black cloud poised in the unbroken centre on a tower shaft of light; he came out of love through a wind full of turning knives and a cave full of flesh-white birds on to a new summit, standing like a stone that faces the stars blowing and stands no ceremony from the sea wind, a hard boy angry on a mound in the middle of a country evening; he put out his chest and said hard words to the world.   Out of love he came marching, head on high, through a cave between two doors to a vantage hall room with an iron view over the earth.   He walked to the last rail before pitch space; though the earth bowled round quickly, he saw every plough crease and beast's print, man track and water drop, comb, crest, and plume mark, dust and death groove and signature and time-cast shade, from icefield to icefield, sea rims to sea centres, all over the apple-shaped ball under the metal rails beyond the living doors.   He saw through the black thumbprint of a man's city to the fossil thumb of a once-lively man of meadows; through the grass and clover fossil of the country print to the whole hand of a forgotten city drowned under Europe; through the handprint to the arm of an empire broken like Venus; through the arm to the breast, from history to the thigh, through the thigh in the dark to the first and West print between the dark and the green Eden; and the garden was undrowned, to this next minute and for ever, under

Asia in the earth that rolled on to its music in the beginning evening. When God was sleeping, he had climbed a ladder, and the room three jumps above the final rung was roofed and floored with the live pages of the book of days; the pages were gardens, the built words were trees, and Eden grew above him into Eden, and Eden grew down to Eden through the lower earth, an endless corridor of boughs and birds and leaves. He stood on a slope no wider than the loving room of the world, and the two poles kissed behind his shoulders; the boy stumbled forward like Atlas, loped over the iron view through the cave of knives and the capsized overgrowths of time to the hill in the field that had been a short mark under the platform in the clouds over the multiplying gardens.

'Wake up,' she said into his ear; the iron characters were broken in her smile, and Eden shrank into the seventh shade. She told him to look in her eyes. He had thought that her eyes were brown or green, but they were sea-blue with black lashes, and her thick hair was black. She rumpled his hair, and put his hand deep in her breast so that he knew the nipple of her heart was red. He looked in her eyes, but they made a round glass of the sun, and as he moved sharply away he saw through the transparent trees; she could make a long crystal of each tree, and turn the house wood into gauze. She told him her name, but he had forgotten it as she spoke; she told him her age, and it was a new number. 'Look in my eyes,' she said. It was only an hour to the proper night, the stars were coming out and the moon was ready. She took his hand and led him racing between trees over the ridge of the dewy hill, over the flowering nettles and the shut grass-flowers, over the silence into sunlight and the noise of a sea breaking on sand and stone.

The hill in a screen of trees: between the incountry fields and the incoming sea, night on the wood and the stained

beach yellow in the sun, the vanishing corn through the ten
dry miles of farmland and the golden wastes where the split
sand lapped over rocks, it stood between time over a secret
root.   The hill in two searchlights: the back moon shone on
seven trees, and the sun of a strange day moved above water
in the spluttering foreground.   The hill between an owl
and a seagull: the boy heard two birds' voices as brown
wings climbed through the branches and the white wings
before him fluttered on the sea waves.   'Tu wit tu woo, do
not adventure any more.'   Now the gulls that swam in the
sky told him to race on along the warm sand until the water
hugged him to its waves and the spindrift tore around him
like a wind and a chain.   The girl had her hand in his, and
she rubbed her cheek on his shoulder.   He was glad of her
near him, for the princess was broken, and the monstrous
girl was turned into a tree, and the frightening girl who
threw the country into a daze of sizes, and drove him out of
love into the cloudy house, was left alone in the moon's
circle and the seven shades behind the screen.

It was hot that morning in the unexpected sunshine.   A
girl dressed in cotton put her mouth to his ear.   'I'll run
you to the sea,' she said, and her breasts jumped up and
down as she raced in front of him, with her hair flying wild,
to the edge of the sea that was not made of water and the
small, thundering pebbles that broke in a million pieces as
the dry sea moved in.   Along the bright wrack-line, from
the horizon where the vast birds sailed like boats, from the
four compass corners, bellying up through the weed beds,
melting from orient and tropic, surging through the ice
hills and the whale grounds, through sunset and sunrise
corridors, the salt gardens and the herring fields, whirlpool
and rock pool, out of the trickle in the mountain, down the
waterfalls, a white-faced sea of people, the terrible mortal
number of the waves, all the centuries' sea drenched in the

hail before Christ, who suffered to-morrow's storm wind,
came in with the whole world's voices on the endless beach.

'Come back! Come back!' the boy cried to the girl.

She ran on unheeding over the sand and was lost among
the sea. Now her face was a white drop of water in the
horizontal rainfall, and her limbs were white as snow and
lost in the white, walking tide. Now the heart in her
breast was a small red bell that rang in a wave, her colourless
hair fringed the spray, and her voice lapped over the flesh-
and-bone water.

He cried again, but she had mingled with the people
moving in and out. Their tides were drawn by a grave
moon that never lost an arc. Their long, sea gestures were
deliberate, the flat hands beckoning, the heads uplifted, the
eyes in the mask faces set in one direction. Oh, where was
she now in the sea? Among the white, walking, and the
coral-eyed. 'Come back! Come back! Darling, run
out of the sea.' Among the processional waves. The bell
in her breast was ringing over the sand.

He ran to the yellow foot of the dunes, calling over his
shoulder. 'Run out of the sea.' In the once-green water
where the fishes swam, where the gulls rested, where the
luminous stones were rubbed and rocked on the scales of
the green bed, when ships puffed over the tradeways, and
the mad, nameless animals came down to drink the salt.
Among the measuring people. Oh, where was she now?
The sea was lost behind the dunes. He stumbled on over
sand and sandflowers like a blind boy in the sun. The sun
dodged round his shoulders.

There was a story once upon a time whispered in the
water voice; it blew out the echo from the trees behind
the beach in the golden hollows, scraped on the wood until
the musical birds and beasts came jumping into sunshine. A
raven flew by him, out of a window in the Flood to the blind,

wind tower shaking in to-morrow's anger like a scarecrow
made out of weathers.

'Once upon a time,' said the water voice.

'Do not adventure any more,' said the echo.

'She is ringing a bell for you in the sea.'

'I am the owl and the echo: you shall never go back.'

On a hill to the horizon stood an old man building a boat,
and the light that slanted from the sea cast the holy mountain
of a shadow over the three-storied decks and the Eastern
timber.   And through the sky, out of the beds and gardens,
down the white precipice built of feathers, the loud combs
and mounds, from the caves in the hill, the cloudy shapes of
birds and beasts and insects drifted into the hewn door.   A
dove with a green petal followed in the raven's flight.   Cool
rain began to fall.

The Lemon

Early one morning, under the arc of a lamp, carefully, silently, in smock and rubber gloves, the doctor grafted a cat's head on to a chicken's trunk. The cat-headed creature, in a house of glass, swayed on its legs; though it stared through the slits of its eyes, it saw nothing; there was the flutter of a strange pulse under its fur and feathers; and, lifting its foot to the right of the glass wall, it rocked again to the left. Change the sex of a dog: it cries like a bitch in a high heat, and sniffs, bewildered, over the blind litter. Such a strange dog, with a grafted ovary, howled in its cage. The doctor put his ear to the glass, hoping for a new sound. The sun blew in through the laboratory windows, and the light of the wind was the colour of the sun. With music in his ears, he moved among the phials and the bottles of life; the mutilated were silent; the new born in the rabbits' cages drew down the hygienic air delightedly into their lungs. To-morrow there were to be mastoids for the ferret by the window, but to-day it leapt in the sun.

The hill was as big as a mountain, and the house swelled like a hill on the topmost peak. Holding too many rooms, the house had a room for the wild owls, and a cellar for the vermin that multiplied on clean straw and grew fat as rabbits. The people in the house moved like too many ghosts among the white-sheeted tables, met face to face in the corridors and covered their eyes for fear of a new stranger, or suddenly crowded together in the central hall, questioning one another as to the names of the new born. One by one the faces vanished, but there was always one to take its place, a woman with a child at her breast, or a blind man from the world. All had possession of the keys of the house.

There was one boy among them who had the name of the house, and, son of the house that was called a hill, he played with the shadows in the corridors and slept at night in a high room shuttered from the stars. But the people of the house slept in sight of the moon; they heard the gulls from the sea, the noise of the waves, when the wind blew from the south, breaking on sand, and slept with their eyes open.

The doctor woke up with the birds, seeing the sun rise each morning in a coloured water, and the day, like the growths in his jars, grow brighter and stronger as the growing hours let the rain or the shine and the particles of winter light fall from them. As was his custom, he turned, this one morning, from the window where the weazel leapt, to the life behind glass. He marked with an unmortal calm, with the never-ended beginning of a smile no mother bared with the mouth of her milk, how the young lapped at their mothers and his creatures, and the newly hatched fluttered, and the papped birds opened their beaks. He was power and the clay knife, he was the sound and the substance, for he made a hand of glass, a hand with a vein, and sewed it upon the flesh, and it strengthened with the heat of the false light, and the glass nails grew long. Life ran from his fingers, in the heat of his acids, on the surface of the boiling herbs; he had death in a thousand powders; he had frozen a crucifix of steam; all the great chemistries of the earth, the mystery of matter—'See,' he said aloud, 'a brand on a frog's forehead where there was neither'—in his room at the top of the house had no mystery.

The house was one mystery. Everything happens in a blaze of light; the groping of the boy's blind hands along the

walls of the corridors was a movement of light, though the
last candle dimmed by the head of the stairs and the lines of
light at the feet of the locked doors were suddenly taken
away.   Nant, the boy, was not alone; he heard a frock
rustle, a hand beneath his own scrape on the distemper.
'Whose hand?' he said softly.   Then, flying in a panic down
the dark carpets, he cried more loudly: 'Never answer me.'
'Your hand,' said the dark, and Nant stopped still.

Death was too long for the doctor, and eternity took too
much time.

I was that boy in a dream, and I stood stock still, knowing
myself to be alone, knowing that the voice was mine and the
dark not the death of the sun but the dark light thrown back
by the walls of the windowless corridors.   I put out my
arm, and it turned into a tree.

Early that morning, under the arc of a lamp, the doctor
made a new acid, turning it round and round with a spoon,
seeing it have colour in its beaker and then, by the change of
heat, be the colour of water.   It was the strongest acid,
burning the air, but it struggled through his fingers sweet as
a syrup and did not burn at all.   Carefully, silently, he
raised the beaker and opened the door of a cage.   This was
a new milk for the cat.   He poured the acid into a saucer,
and the cat-headed creature slipped down to drink.   I was
that cat-head in a dream; I drank the acid, and I slept; I woke
up in death, but there I forgot the dream and moved on a
different being in the image of the boy who was terrified of
the dark.   And, my arm no longer the branch of a tree,
like a mole I hurried from light and to the light; for one
blind moment I was a mole with a child's hands digging, up
or down, I knew not which, in the Welsh earth.   I knew
that I was dreaming, but suddenly I awoke to the hard, real
lack of light in the corridors of the house.   There was
nobody to guide me; the doctor, the foreigner in a white

coat making a new logic in his tower of birds, was my only friend. Nant raced for the doctor's tower. Up spiral stairs and a broken ladder, reading, by candle, a sign that said To London and the Sun, he climbed in my image, I in his, and we were two brothers climbing.

The key was on a chain ringed from my waist. Opening the door, I found the doctor as I always found him, staring through the walls of a glass cage. He smiled but paid no heed to me who had lusted a hundred seconds for his smile and his white coat. 'I gave it my acid and it died,' the doctor said. 'And, after ten minutes, the dead hen rose to its feet; it rubbed against glass like a cat, and I saw its cat's head. This was ten minutes' death.'

A storm came up, black bodied, from the sea, bringing rain and twelve winds to drive the hillbirds off the face of the sky; the storm, the black man, the whistler from the sea bottom and the fringe of the fish stones, the thunder, the lightning, the mighty pebbles, these came up; as a sickness, an afterbirth, coming up from the belly of weathers; mad as a mist coming up, the antichrist from a seaflame or a steam crucifix, coming up the putting on of rain; as the acid was stronger, the multiplying storm, the colour of temper, the whole, the unholy, rock-handed, came up coming up.

This was the exterior world.

And the shadows, that were web and cloven footed in the house, with the beaks of birds, the shifted shadows that bore a woman in each hand, had no casting substances; and the foam horses of the exterior sea climbed like foxes on the hills. This that held Nant and the doctor, the bone of a horse head, the ox and black man arising from the clay picture, was the interior world. This was the interior world where the acid grew stronger, and the death in the acid added ten days to the dead time.

Still the doctor did not see me. I who was the doctor in

a dream, the foreign logician, the maker of birds, engrossed
in the acid strengthening and the search for oblivion, soon
raised the beaker to my mouth as the storm came up.
There was thunder as I drank; and, as he fell, the lightning
crossed on the wind.

'There is a dead man in the tower,' a woman said to her
companion as they stood by the door of the central hall.

'There is a dead man in the tower,' said the corner
echoes, and their voices rose through the house. Suddenly
the hall was crowded, and the people of the house moved
among one another, questioning as to the name of the new
dead.

Nant stood over the doctor. Now the doctor was dead.
There was a corridor leading to the tower of ten days' death,
and there a woman danced alone, with the hands of a man
upon her shoulders. And soon the virgins joined her,
bared to the waist, and made the movements of dancing;
they danced towards the open doors of the corridors, stood
lightly in the doorways; they danced four steps towards the
doors, and then danced four steps away. In the long hall
they danced in celebration of the dead. This was the dance
of the halt, the blind, and the half dead, this the dance of the
abnegation of the dead, this the dance of the children, the
grave girls bared to the waist, this the dance of the dreamers,
the open-eyed and the naked hopheads, sleeping as they
moved. The doctor was dead at my feet. I knelt down
to count his ribs, to raise his jaw, to take the beaker of acid
from his hand. But the dead hand stiffened.

Said a voice at my elbow: 'Unlock the hand.' I moved
to obey the voice, but a softer voice said at my ear: 'Let
the hand stiffen.' 'Strike the second voice.' 'Strike the first
voice.' 'Unlock the hand.' 'Let the hand stiffen.' I struck
at the two voices with my fist, and Nant's hand turned into
a tree.

At noon the storm was stronger; all afternoon it shook the tower, pulling the slates from the roof; it came from the sea and the earth from the sea beds and the roots of the forests. I could hear nothing but the voice of the thunder that drowned the two stricken voices; I saw the lightning stride up the hill, a bright, forked man blinding me through the tower windows. And still they danced, into the early evening, the storm increasing, and still the half-naked virgins danced to the doors. This was the dance of the celebration of death in the interior world.

I heard a voice say over the thunder: 'The dead shall be buried. This was not everlasting death, but a death of days; this was a sleep with no heart. We bury the dead,' said the voice that heard my heart, the brief and the everlasting. The storm up the wind measured off the distances of the voice, but a lull in the rain let the two struggling voices at my side recall me to the hand and the acid. I dragged up the stiffening hand, unlocked the fingers, and raised the beaker to my mouth. As the glass burned me, there came a knocking at the door and a cry from the people of the house. They who were seeking the body of the new dead worried the door. My boy's heart was breaking. Swiftly I glanced towards the table where a lemon lay on a plate. I punctured the skin of the lemon, and poured in the acid. Then down came the storm of the dark voices and the knocks, and the tower door broke on its hinges. The dead was found. I fought between the shoulders of the entering strangers and, leaving them to their picking, spiralled down, sped through the corridors, the lemon at my breast.

Nant and I were brothers in this wild world far from the border villages, from the sea that has England in its hand, from the lofty spires and the uneaten graves beneath them. As one, one-headed, two-footed, we ran through the passages and the halls, seeing no shadows, hearing none of the wicked intimacies of the house. The rooms were empty of wickedness. We looked for a devil in the corners, but their secrets were ours. So we ran on, afraid of our footfalls, exulting in the beating of the blood, for death was at our breast, a sharp fruit, a full and yellow tumour shaped to the skin. Nant was a lonely runner in the house; I parted from him, leaving a half ache and a half terror, going my own way, the way of the light breaking over Cathmarw hill and the Black Valley. And, going his own way, he climbed alone up a stone stairs to the last tower. He put his mouth to her cheek and touched her nipple. The storm died as she touched him.

He cut the lemon in half with the scissors dangling from the rope of her skirt.

And the storm came up as they drank.

This was the coming of death in the interior world.

After the Fair

THE fair was over, the lights in the coco-nut stalls were put out, and the wooden horses stood still in the darkness, waiting for the music and the hum of the machines that would set them trotting forward. One by one, in every booth, the naphtha jets were turned down and the canvases pulled over the little gaming tables. The crowd went home, and there were lights in the windows of the caravans.

Nobody had noticed the girl. In her black clothes she stood against the side of the roundabouts, hearing the last feet tread upon the sawdust and the last voices die in the distance. Then, all alone on the deserted ground, surrounded by the shapes of wooden horses and cheap fairy boats, she looked for a place to sleep. Now here and now there, she raised the canvas that shrouded the coco-nut stalls and peered into the warm darkness. She was frightened to step inside, and as a mouse scampered across the littered shavings on the floor, or as the canvas creaked and a rush of wind set it dancing, she ran away and hid again near the roundabouts. Once she stepped on the boards; the bells round a horse's throat jingled and were still; she did not dare breathe again until all was quiet and the darkness had forgotten the noise of the bells. Then here and there she went peeping for a bed, into each gondola, under each tent. But there was nowhere, nowhere in all the fair for her to sleep. One place was too silent, and in another was the noise of mice. There was straw in the corner of the Astrologer's tent, but it moved as she touched it; she knelt by its side and put out her hand; she felt a baby's hand upon her own.

Now there was nowhere, so slowly she turned towards the caravans on the outskirts of the field, and found all but two to be unlit. She waited, clutching her empty bag, and wondering which caravan she should disturb. At last she decided to knock upon the window of the little, shabby one near her, and, standing on tiptoes, she looked in. The fattest man she had ever seen was sitting in front of the stove, toasting a piece of bread. She tapped three times on the glass, then hid in the shadows. She heard him come to the top of the steps and call out 'Who? Who?' but she dare not answer. 'Who? Who?' he called again.

She laughed at his voice which was as thin as he was fat.

He heard her laughter and turned to where the darkness concealed her. 'First you tap,' he said, 'then you hide, then you laugh.'

She stepped into the circle of light, knowing she need no longer hide herself.

'A girl,' he said. 'Come in, and wipe your feet.' He did not wait but retreated into his caravan, and she could do nothing but follow him up the steps and into the crowded room. He was seated again, and toasting the same piece of bread. 'Have you come in?' he said, for his back was towards her.

'Shall I close the door?' she asked, and closed it before he replied.

She sat on the bed and watched him toast the bread until it burnt.

'I can toast better than you,' she said.

'I don't doubt it,' said the Fat Man.

She watched him put the charred toast upon a plate by his side, take another round of bread and hold that, too, in front of the stove. It burnt very quickly.

'Let me toast it for you,' she said.   Ungraciously he handed her the fork and the loaf.

'Cut it,' he said, 'toast it, and eat it.'

She sat on the chair.

'See the dent you've made on my bed,' said the Fat Man. 'Who are you to come in and dent my bed?'

'My name is Annie,' she told him.

Soon all the bread was toasted and buttered, so she put it in the centre of the table and arranged two chairs.

'I'll have mine on the bed,' said the Fat Man.   'You'll have it here.'

When they had finished their supper, he pushed back his chair and stared at her across the table.

'I am the Fat Man,' he said.   'My home is Treorchy; the Fortune-Teller next door is Aberdare.'

'I am nothing to do with the fair,' she said, 'I am Cardiff.'

'There's a town,' agreed the Fat Man.   He asked her why she had come away.

'Money,' said Annie.

Then he told her about the fair and the places he had been to and the people he had met.   He told her his age and his weight and the names of his brothers and what he would call his son.   He showed her a picture of Boston Harbour and the photograph of his mother who lifted weights.   He told her how summer looked in Ireland.

'I've always been a fat man,' he said, 'and now I'm the Fat Man; there's nobody to touch me for fatness.'   He told her of a heat-wave in Sicily and of the Mediterranean Sea. She told him of the baby in the Astrologer's tent.

'That's the stars again,' he said.

'The baby'll die,' said Annie.

He opened the door and walked out into the darkness. She looked about her but did not move, wondering if he had gone to fetch a policeman.   It would never do to be caught by the policeman again. She stared through the open door into the inhospitable night and drew her chair closer to the stove.

'Better to be caught in the warmth,' she said. But she trembled at the sound of the Fat Man approaching, and pressed her hands upon her thin breast as he climbed up the steps like a walking mountain. She could see him smile through the darkness.

'See what the stars have done,' he said, and brought in the Astrologer's baby in his arms.

After she had nursed it against her and it had cried on the bosom of her dress, she told him how she had feared his going.

'What should I be doing with a policeman?'

She told him that the policeman wanted her. 'What have you done for a policeman to be wanting you?'

She did not answer but took the child nearer to her wasted breast. He saw her thinness.

'You must eat, Cardiff,' he said.

Then the child began to cry. From a little wail its voice rose into a tempest of despair. The girl rocked it to and fro on her lap, but nothing soothed it.

'Stop it! Stop it!' said the Fat Man, and the tears increased. Annie smothered it in kisses, but it howled again.

'We must do something,' she said.

'Sing it a lullaby.'

She sang, but the child did not like her singing.

'There's only one thing,' said Annie, 'we must take it on the roundabouts.' With the child's arm around her neck she stumbled down the steps and ran towards the deserted fair, the Fat Man panting behind her.

She found her way through the tents and stalls into the centre of the ground where the wooden horses stood waiting, and clambered up on to a saddle. 'Start the

engine,' she called out.   In the distance the Fat Man could
be heard cranking up the antique machine that drove the
horses all the day into a wooden gallop.   She heard the
spasmodic humming of the engines; the boards rattled under
the horses' feet.   She saw the Fat Man get up by her side,
pull the central lever, and climb on to the saddle of the
smallest horse of all.   As the roundabout started, slowly at
first and slowly gaining speed, the child at the girl's breast
stopped crying and clapped its hands.   The night wind tore
through its hair, the music jangled in its ears.   Round and
round the wooden horses sped, drowning the cries of the
wind with the beating of their hooves.

And so the men from the caravans found them, the Fat
Man and the girl in black with a baby in her arms, racing
round and round on their mechanical steeds to the ever-
increasing music of the organ.

The Visitor

His hands were weary, though all night they had lain over the sheets of his bed and he had moved them only to his mouth and his wild heart. The veins ran, unhealthily blue streams, into the white sea. Milk at his side steamed out of a chipped cup. He smelt the morning, and knew that cocks in the yard were putting back their heads and crowing at the sun. What were the sheets around him if not the covering sheets of the dead? What was the busy-voiced clock, sounding between photographs of mother and dead wife, if not the voice of an old enemy? Time was merciful enough to let the sun shine on his bed, and merciless to chime the sun away when night came over and even more he needed the red light and the clear heat.

Rhianon was attendant on a dead man, and put the chipped edge of the cup to a dead lip. It could not be heart that beat under the ribs. Hearts do not beat in the dead. While he had lain ready for the inch-tape and the acid, Rhianon had cut open his chest with a book-knife, torn out the heart, put in the clock. He heard her say, for the third time, 'Drink the lovely milk.' And, feeling it run sour over his tongue, and her hand caress his forehead, he knew he was not dead. He was a living man. For many miles the months flowed into the years, rounding the dry days.

Callaghan to-day would sit and talk with him. He heard in his brain the voices of Callaghan and Rhianon battle until he slept, and tasted the blood of words. His hands were weary. He brooded over his long, white body, marking the ribs stick through the sides. The hands had held other

25

hands and thrown a ball high into the air.   Now they were
dead hands.   He could wind them about his hair and let
them rest untingling on his belly or lose them in the valley
between Rhianon's breasts.   It did not matter what he did
with them.   They were as dead as the hands of the clock,
and moved to clockwork.

'Shall I close the windows until the sun's warmer?'
said Rhianon.

'I'm not cold.'

He would tell her that the dead feel neither cold nor
warmth, sun and wind could never penetrate his cloths.
But she would laugh in her kind way and kiss him on the
forehead and say to him, 'Peter, what's getting you down?
You'll be out and about one day.'

One day he would walk on the Jarvis hills like a boy's
ghost, and hear the people say: 'There walks the ghost of
Peter, a poet, who was dead for years before they buried
him.'

Rhianon tucked the sheets around his shoulders, gave him
a morning kiss, and carried the chipped cup away.

A man with a brush had drawn a rib of colour under the
sun and painted many circles around the circle of the sun.
Death was a man with a scythe, but that summer day no
living stalk was to be cut down.

The invalid waited for his visitor.   Peter waited for
Callaghan.   His room was a world within a world.   A
world in him went round and round, and a sun rose in him
and a moon fell.   Callaghan was the west wind, and
Rhianon blew away the chills of the west wind like a wind
from Tahiti.

He let his hand rest on his head, stone on stone.   Never
had the voice of Rhianon been so remote as when it told
him that the sour milk was lovely.   What was she but a
sweetheart talking madly to her sweetheart under a coffin of

garments? Somebody in the night had turned him up and emptied him of all but a false heart. That under the ribs' armour was not his, not his the beating of a vein in the foot. His arms could no longer make their movements nor a circle around a girl to shield her from winds and robbers. There was nothing more remote under the sun than his own name, and poetry was a string of words stringed on a beanstick. With his lips he rounded a little ball of sound into some shape, and spoke a word.

There was no to-morrow for dead men. He could not think that after the next night and its sleeping, life would sprout up again like a flower through a coffin's cracks.

His room around him was a vast place. From their frames the lying likenesses of women looked down on him. That was the face of his mother, that nearly yellow oval in its frame of old gold and thinning hair. And, next to her, dead Mary. Though Callaghan blew hard, the walls around Mary would never fall down. He thought of her as she had been, remembered her Peter, darling, Peter, and her smiling eyes.

He remembered he had not smiled since that night, seven years ago, when his heart had trembled so violently within him that he had fallen to the ground. There had been strengthening in the unbelievable setting of the sun. Over the hills and the roof went the broad moons, and summer came after spring. How had he lived at all when Callaghan had not blown away the webs of the world with a great shout, and Millicent spread her loveliness about him? But the dead need no friends. He peered over the turned coffin-lid. Stiff and straight, a man of wax stared back. Taking away the pennies from those dead eyes, he looked on his own face.

'Breed, cardboard on cardboard,' he had cried, 'before I blow down your paste huts with one bellow out of my lungs.' When Mary came, there was nothing between the changing of the days but the divinity he had built around her. His child killed Mary in her womb. He felt his body turn to vapour, and men who had been light as air walked, metal-hooved, through and beyond him.

He started to cry: 'Rhianon, Rhianon, someone has upped and kicked me in the side. Drip, drip, goes my blood in me. Rhianon,' he cried.

She hurried upstairs, and time and time over again wiped away the tears from his cheeks with the sleeve of her dress.

He lay still as the morning matured and grew up into a noble noon. Rhianon passed in and out, her dress, he smelt as she bent over him, smelling of clover and milk. With a new surprise he followed her cool movements around the room, the sweep of her hands as she brushed the dead Mary in her frame. With such surprise, he thought, do the dead follow the movements of the quick, seeing the bloom under the living skin. She should be singing as she moved from mantelpiece to window, putting things right, or should be humming like a bee about her work. But if she had spoken, or laughed, or struck her nails against the thin metal of the candlesticks, drawing forth a bellnote, or if the room had been suddenly crowded with the noises of birds, he would have wept again. It pleased him to look upon the unmoving waves of the bedclothes, and think himself an island set somewhere in the south sea. Upon this island of rich and miraculous plants, the seeds grown fruits hung from the trees and, smaller than apples, dropped with the pacific winds on to the ground to lie there and be the harbourers of the summer slugs.

And thinking of the island set somewhere in the south caverns, he thought of water and longed for water. Rhianon's dress, rustling about her, made the soft noise of water. He called her over to him and touched the bosom of her dress, feeling the water on his hands. 'Water,' he told her, and told her how, as a boy, he had lain on the rocks, his fingers tracing cool shapes on the surfaces of the pools. She brought him water in a glass, and held the glass up level with his eyes so that he could see the room through a wall of water. He did not drink, and she set the glass aside. He imagined the coolness under the sea. Now, on a summer day soon after noon, he wished again for water to close utterly around him, to be no island set above the water but a green place under, staring around a dizzy cavern. He thought of some cool words, and made a line about an olive-tree that grew under a lake. But the tree was a tree of words, and the lake rhymed with another word.

'Sit and read to me, Rhianon.'

'After you have eaten,' she said, and brought him food. He could not think that she had gone down into the kitchen and, with her own hands, prepared his meal. She had gone and had returned with food, as simply as a maiden out of the Old Testament. Her name meant nothing. It was a cool sound. She had a strange name out of the Bible. Such a woman had washed the body after it had been taken off the tree, with cool and competent fingers that touched on the holes like ten blessings. He could cry out to her: 'Put a sweet herb under my arm. With your spittle make me fragrant.'

'What shall I read you?' she asked when at last she sat by his side.

He shook his head, not caring what she read so long as he could hear her speak and think of nothing but the inflections of her voice.

'Ah! gentle may I lay me down, and gentle rest my head,
And gentle sleep the sleep of death, and gentle hear the voice
Of Him that walketh in the garden in the evening time.'

She read on until the Worm sat on the Lily's leaf.

Death lay over his limbs again, and he closed his eyes.

There was no ease from pain nor from the figures of death that went about their familiar business even in the darkness of the heavy lids.

'Shall I kiss you awake?' said Callaghan. His hand was cold on Peter's hand.

'And all the lepers kissed,' said Peter, and fell to wondering what he had meant.

Rhianon saw that he was no longer listening to her, and went on tiptoes away.

Callaghan, left alone, leant over the bed and spread the soft ends of his fingers on Peter's eyes. 'Now it is night,' he said. 'Where shall we go to-night?'

Peter opened his eyes again, saw the spreading fingers and the candles glowing like the heads of poppies. A fear and a blessing were on the room.

The candles must not be blown out, he thought. There must be light, light, light. Wick and wax must never be low. All day and all night the three candles, like three girls, must blush over my bed. These three girls must shelter me.

The first flame danced and then went out. Over the second and the third flame Callaghan pursed his grey mouth. The room was dark. 'Where shall we go to-night?' he said, but waited for no answer, pulling the sheets back from the bed and lifting Peter in his arms. His coat was damp and sweet on Peter's face.

'Oh, Callaghan, Callaghan,' said Peter with his mouth pressed on the black cloth. He felt the movements of Callaghan's body, the tense, the relaxing muscles, the curving of the shoulders, the impact of the feet on the racing earth. A wind from under the clay and the limes of the earth swept up to his hidden face. Only when the boughs

of trees scraped on his back did he know that he was naked.
So that he might not cry aloud, he shut his lips firmly
together over a damp fold of flesh. Callaghan, too, was
naked as a baby.

'Are we naked? We have our bones and our organs, our
skin and our flesh. There is a ribbon of blood tied in your
hair. Do not be frightened. You have a cloth of veins
around your thighs.' The world charged past them, the
wind dropped to nothing, blowing the fruits of battle under
the moon. Peter heard the songs of birds, but no such
songs as he had heard the birds, on his bedroom sill, fetch
out of their throats. The birds were blind.

'Are they blind?' said Callaghan. 'They have worlds in
their eyes. There is white and black in their whistling.
Do not be frightened. There are bright eyes under the
shells of their eggs.'

He came suddenly to a stop, Peter light as a feather in his
arms, and set him gently down on a green globe of soil.
Below there was a valley journeying far away with its burden
of lame trees and grass into the distance where the moon
hung on a navelstring from the dark. From the woods on
either side came the sharp cracks of guns and the pheasants
falling like a rain. But soon the night was silent, softening
the triggers of the fallen twigs that had snapped out under
Callaghan's feet.

Peter, conscious of his sick heart, put a hand to his side
but felt none of the protecting flesh. The tips of his
fingers tingled around the driving blood, but the veins were
invisible. He was dead. Now he knew he was dead.
The ghost of Peter, wound invisible about the ghost of the
blood, stood on his globe and wondered at the corrupting
night.

'What is this valley?' said Peter's voice.

'The Jarvis valley,' said Callaghan. Callaghan, too, was

dead.   Not a bone or a hair stood up under the steadily falling frost.

'This is no Jarvis valley.'

'This is the naked valley.'

The moon, doubling and redoubling the strength of her beams, lit up the barks and the roots and the branches of the Jarvis trees, the busy lice in the wood, the shapes of the stones and the black ants travelling under them, the pebbles in the streams, the secret grass, the untiring death-worms under the blades.   From their holes in the flanks of the hills came the rats and weasels, hairs white in the moon, breeding and struggling as they rushed downward to set their teeth in the cattle's throats.   No sooner did the cattle fall sucked on to the earth and the weasels race away, than all the flies, rising from the dung of the fields, came up like a fog and settled on the sides.   There from the stripped valley rose the smell of death, widening the mountainous nostrils on the face of the moon.   Now the sheep fell and the flies were at them.   The rats and the weasels, fighting over the flesh, dropped one by one with a wound for the sheep's fleas staring out of their hair.   It was to Peter but a little time before the dead, picked to the symmetrical bone, were huddled in under the soil by the wind that blew louder and harder as the fat flies dropped on to the grass.   Now the worm and the death-beetle undid the fibres of the animal bones, worked at them brightly and minutely, and the weeds through the sockets and the flowers on the vanished breasts sprouted up with the colours of the dead life fresh on their leaves.   And the blood that had flowed flowed over the ground, strengthening the blades of the grass, fulfilling the wind-planted seeds in its course, into the mouth of the spring.   Suddenly all the streams were red with blood, a score of winding veins all over the twenty fields, thick with their clotted pebbles.

Peter, in his ghost, cried out with joy. There was life in the naked valley, life in his nakedness. He saw the streams and the beating water, how the flowers shot out of the dead, and the blades and roots were doubled in their power under the stride of the spilt blood.

And the streams stopped. Dust of the dead blew over the spring, and the mouth was choked. Dust lay over the waters like a dark ice. Light, that had been all-eyed and moving, froze in the beams of the moon.

Life in this nakedness, mocked Callaghan at his side, and Peter knew that he was pointing, with the ghost of a finger, down on to the dead streams. But as he spoke, and the shape that Peter's heart had taken in the time of the tangible flesh was aware of the knocks of terror, a life burst out of the pebbles like the thousand lives, wrapped in a boy's body, out of the womb. The streams again went on their way, and the light of the moon, in a new splendour, shone on the valley and magnified the shadows of the valley and pulled the moles and the badgers out of their winter into the deathless midnight season of the world.

'Light breaks over the hill,' said Callaghan, and lifted the invisible Peter in his arms. Dawn, indeed, was breaking far over the Jarvis wilderness still naked under the descending moon.

As Callaghan raced along the rim of the hills and into the woods and over an exultant country where the trees raced with him, Peter cried out joyfully.

He heard Callaghan's laughter like a rattle of thunder that the wind took up and doubled. There was a shouting in the wind, a commotion under the surface of the earth. Now under the roots and now on the tops of the wild trees, he and his stranger were racing against the cock. Over and under the falling fences of the light they climbed and shouted.

'Listen to the cock,' cried Peter, and the sheets of the bed rolled up to his chin.

A man with a brush had drawn a red rib down the east. The ghost of a circle around the circle of the moon spun through a cloud. He passed his tongue over his lips that had miraculously clothed themselves with skin and flesh. In his mouth was a strange taste, as if last night, three hundred nights ago, he had squeezed the head of a poppy and drunk and slept. There was the old rumour of Callaghan down his brain. From dawn to dark he had talked of death, had seen a moth caught in the candle, had heard the laughter that could not have been his ring in his ears. The cock cried again, and a bird whistled like a scythe through wheat.

Rhianon, with a sweet, naked throat, stepped into the room.

'Rhianon,' he said, 'hold my hand, Rhianon.'

She did not hear him, but stood over his bed and fixed him with an unbreakable sorrow.

'Hold my hand,' he said.   And then: 'Why are you putting the sheet over my face?'

The Enemies

It was morning in the green acres of the Jarvis valley, and
Mr Owen was picking the weeds from the edges of his
garden path. A great wind pulled at his beard, the vegetable world roared under his feet. A rook had lost itself in
the sky, and was making a noise to its mate; but the mate
never came, and the rook flew into the west with a woe in its
beak. Mr Owen, who had stood up to ease his shoulders
and look at the sky, observed how dark the wings beat
against the red sun. In her draughty kitchen Mrs Owen
grieved over the soup. Once, in past days, the valley had
housed the cattle alone; the farm-boys came down from the
hills to holla at the cattle and to drive them to be milked;
but no stranger set foot in the valley. Mr Owen, walking
lonely through the country, had come upon it at the end of a
late summer evening when the cattle were lying down still,
and the stream that divided it was speaking over the pebbles.
Here, thought Mr Owen, I will build a small house with one
storey, in the middle of the valley, set around by a garden.
And, remembering clearly the way he had come along the
winding hills, he returned to his village and the questions of
Mrs Owen. So it came about that a house with one storey
was built in the green fields; a garden was dug and planted,
and a low fence put up around the garden to keep the cows
from the vegetables.

That was early in the year. Now summer and autumn
had gone over; the garden had blossomed and died; there
was frost at the weeds. Mr Owen bent down again,
tidying the path, while the wind blew back the heads of the

35

nearby grasses and made an oracle of each green mouth. Patiently he strangled the weeds; up came the roots, making war in the soil around them; insects were busy in the holes where the weeds had sprouted, but, dying between his fingers, they left no stain. He grew tired of their death, and tireder of the fall of the weeds. Up came the roots, down went the cheap, green heads.

Mrs Owen, peering into the depths of her crystal, had left the soup to bubble on unaided. The ball grew dark, then lightened as a rainbow moved within it. Growing hot like a sun, and cooling again like an arctic star, it shone in the folds of her dress where she held it lovingly. The tea-leaves in her cup at breakfast had told of a dark stranger. What would the crystal tell her? Mrs Owen wondered.

Up came the roots, and a crooked worm, disturbed by the probing of the fingers, wriggled blind in the sun. Of a sudden the valley filled all its hollows with the wind, with the voice of the roots, with the breathing of the nether sky. Not only a mandrake screams; torn roots have their cries; each weed Mr Owen pulled out of the ground screamed like a baby. In the village behind the hill the wind would be raging, the clothes on the garden lines would be set to strange dances. And women with shapes in their wombs would feel a new knocking as they bent over the steamy tubs. Life would go on in the veins, in the bones, the binding flesh, that had their seasons and their weathers even as the valley binding the house about with the flesh of the green grass.

The ball, like an open grave, gave up its dead to Mrs Owen. She stared on the lips of women and the hairs of men that wound into a pattern on the face of the crystal world. But suddenly the patterns were swept away, and she could see nothing but the shapes of the Jarvis hills. A man with a black hat was walking down the paths into the invisible valley beneath. If he walked any nearer he would fall into her lap. 'There's a man with a black hat walking on the hills,' she called through the window. Mr Owen smiled and went on weeding.

It was at this time that the Reverend Mr Davies lost his way; he had been losing it most of the morning, but now he had lost it altogether, and stood perturbed under a tree on the rim of the Jarvis hills. A great wind blew through the branches, and a great grey-green earth moved unsteadily beneath him. Wherever he looked the hills stormed up to the sky, and wherever he sought to hide from the wind he was frightened by the darkness. The farther he walked, the stranger was the scenery around him; it rose to undreamed-of heights, and then fell down again into a valley no bigger than the palm of his hand. And the trees walked like men. By a divine coincidence he reached the rim of the hills just as the sun reached the centre of the sky. With the wide world rocking from horizon to horizon, he stood under a tree and looked down into the valley. In the fields was a little house with a garden. The valley roared around it, the wind leapt at it like a boxer, but the house stood still. To Mr Davies it seemed as though the house had been carried out of a village by a large bird and placed in the very middle of the tumultuous universe.

But as he climbed over the craggy edges and down the side of the hill, he lost his place in Mrs Owen's crystal. A cloud displaced his black hat, and under the cloud walked a very old phantom, a shape of air with stars all frozen in its beard, and a half-moon for a smile. Mr Davies knew nothing of this as the stones scratched his hands. He was old, he was drunk with the wine of the morning, but the stuff that came out of his cuts was a human blood.

Nor did Mr Owen, with his face near the soil and his hands on the necks of the screaming weeds, know of the transformation in the crystal. He had heard Mrs Owen prophesy the coming of the black hat, and had smiled as he always smiled at her faith in the powers of darkness. He had looked up when she called, and, smiling, had returned to the clearer call of the ground. 'Multiply, multiply,' he had said to the worms disturbed in their channelling, and had cut the brown worms in half so that the halves might breed and spread their life over the garden and go out, contaminating, into the fields and the bellies of the cattle.

Of this Mr Davies knew nothing. He saw a young man with a beard bent industriously over the garden soil; he saw that the house was a pretty picture, with the face of a pale young woman pressed up against the window. And, removing his black hat, he introduced himself as the rector of a village some ten miles away.

'You are bleeding,' said Mr Owen.

Mr Davies's hands, indeed, were covered in blood.

When Mrs Owen had seen to the rector's cuts, she sat him down in the arm-chair near the window, and made him a strong cup of tea.

'I saw you on the hill,' she said, and he asked her how she had seen him, for the hills are high and a long way off.

'I have good eyes,' she answered.

He did not doubt her. Her eyes were the strangest he had seen.

'It is quiet here,' said Mr Davies.

'We have no clock,' she said, and laid the table for three.

'You are very kind.'

'We are kind to those that come to us.'

He wondered how many came to the lonely house in the valley, but did not question her for fear of what she would reply. He guessed she was an uncanny woman loving the dark because it was dark. He was too old to question the secrets of darkness, and now, with the black suit torn and

wet and his thin hands bound with the bandages of the
stranger woman, he felt older than ever.   The winds of the
morning might blow him down, and the sudden dropping of
the dark be blind in his eyes.   Rain might pass through him
as it passes through the body of a ghost.   A tired, white-
haired old man, he sat under the window, almost invisible
against the panes and the white cloth of the chair.

Soon the meal was ready, and Mr Owen came in unwashed
from the garden.

'Shall I say grace?' asked Mr Davies when all three were
seated around the table.

Mrs Owen nodded.

'O Lord God Almighty, bless this our meal,' said Mr
Davies.   Looking up as he continued his prayer, he saw that
Mr and Mrs Owen had closed their eyes.   'We thank Thee
for the bounties that Thou hast given us.'   And he saw that
the lips of Mr and Mrs Owen were moving softly.   He could
not hear what they said, but he knew that the prayers they
spoke were not his prayers.

'Amen,' said all three together.

Mr Owen, proud in his eating, bent over the plate as he
had bent over the complaining weeds.   Outside the window
was the brown body of the earth, the green skin of the grass,
and the breasts of the Jarvis hills; there was a wind that
chilled the animal earth, and a sun that had drunk up the
dews on the fields; there was creation sweating out of the
pores of the trees; and the grains of sand on far-away sea-
shores would be multiplying as the sea rolled over them.
He felt the coarse foods on his tongue; there was a meaning
in the rind of the meat, and a purpose in the lifting of food
to mouth.   He saw, with a sudden satisfaction, that Mrs
Owen's throat was bare.

She, too, was bent over her plate, but was letting the
teeth of her fork nibble at the corners of it.   She did not

eat, for the old powers were upon her, and she dared not lift up her head for the greenness of her eyes. She knew by the sound which way the wind blew in the valley; she knew the stage of the sun by the curve of the shadows on the cloth. Oh, that she could take her crystal, and see within it the stretches of darkness covering up this winter light. But there was a darkness gathering in her mind, drawing in the light around her. There was a ghost on her left; with all her strength she drew in the intangible light that moved around him, and mixed it in her dark brains.

Mr Davies, like a man sucked by a bird, felt desolation in his veins, and, in a sweet delirium, told of his adventures on the hills, of how it had been cold and blowing, and how the hills went up and down. He had been lost, he said, and had found a dark retreat to shelter from the bullies in the wind; but the darkness had frightened him, and he had walked again on the hills where the morning tossed him about like a ship on the sea. Wherever he went he was blown in the open or frightened in the narrow shades. There was nowhere, he said pityingly, for an old man to go. Loving his parish, he had loved the surrounding lands, but the hills had given under his feet or plunged him into the air. And, loving his God, he had loved the darkness where men of old had worshipped the dark invisible. But now the hill caves were full of shapes and voices that mocked him because he was old.

'He is frightened of the dark,' thought Mrs Owen, 'the lovely dark.' With a smile, Mr Owen thought: 'He is frightened of the worm in the earth, of the copulation in the tree, of the living grease in the soil.' They looked at the old man, and saw that he was more ghostly than ever. The window behind him cast a ragged circle of light round his head.

Suddenly Mr Davies knelt down to pray. He did not

understand the cold in his heart nor the fear that bewildered him as he knelt, but, speaking his prayers for deliverance, he stared up at the shadowed eyes of Mrs Owen and at the smiling eyes of her husband. Kneeling on the carpet at the head of the table, he stared in bewilderment at the dark mind and the gross dark body. He stared and he prayed, like an old god beset by his enemies.

The Tree

Rising from the house that faced the Jarvis hills in the long distance, there was a tower for the day-birds to build in and for the owls to fly around at night. From the village the light in the tower window shone like a glow-worm through the panes; but the room under the sparrows' nests was rarely lit; webs were spun over its unwashed ceilings; it stared over twenty miles of the up-and-down county, and the corners kept their secrets where there were claw marks in the dust.

The child knew the house from roof to cellar; he knew the irregular lawns and the gardener's shed where flowers burst out of their jars; but he could not find the key that opened the door of the tower.

The house changed to his moods, and a lawn was the sea or the shore or the sky or whatever he wished it. When a lawn was a sad mile of water, and he was sailing on a broken flower down the waves, the gardener would come out of his shed near the island of bushes. He too would take a stalk, and sail. Straddling a garden broom, he would fly wherever the child wished. He knew every story from the beginning of the world.

'In the beginning,' he would say, 'there was a tree.'

'What kind of a tree?'

'The tree where that blackbird's whistling.'

'A hawk, a hawk,' cried the child.

The gardener would look up at the tree, seeing a monstrous hawk perched on a bough or an eagle swinging in the wind.

The gardener loved the Bible. When the sun sank and the garden was full of people, he would sit with a candle in his shed, reading of the first love and the legend of apples and serpents. But the death of Christ on a tree he loved most. Trees made a fence around him, and he knew of the changing of the seasons by the hues on the bark and the rushing of sap through the covered roots. His world moved and changed as spring moved along the branches, changing their nakedness; his God grew up like a tree from the apple-shaped earth, giving bud to His children and letting His children be blown from their places by the breezes of winter; winter and death moved in one wind. He would sit in his shed and read of the crucifixion, looking over the jars on his window-shelf into the winter nights. He would think that love fails on such nights, and that many of its children are cut down.

The child transfigured the blowsy lawns with his playing. The gardener called him by his mother's name, and seated him on his knee, and talked to him of the wonders of Jerusalem and the birth in the manger.

'In the beginning was the village of Bethlehem,' he whispered to the child before the bell rang for tea out of the growing darkness.

'Where is Bethlehem?'

'Far away,' said the gardener, 'in the East.'

To the east stood the Jarvis hills, hiding the sun, their trees drawing up the moon out of the grass.

The child lay in bed. He watched the rocking-horse and wished that it would grow wings so that he could mount it and ride into the Arabian sky. But the winds of Wales blew at the curtains, and crickets made a noise in the untidy plot under the window. His toys were dead. He started to cry and then stopped, knowing no reason for tears. The night was windy and cold, he was warm under the sheets; the night was as big as a hill, he was a boy in bed.

Closing his eyes, he stared into a spinning cavern deeper than the darkness of the garden where the first tree on which the unreal birds had fastened stood alone and bright as fire. The tears ran back under his lids as he thought of the first tree that was planted so near him, like a friend in the garden. He crept out of bed and tiptoed to the door. The rocking-horse bounded forward on its springs, startling the child into a noiseless scamper back to bed. The child looked at the horse and the horse was quiet; he tiptoed again along the carpet, and reached the door, and turned the knob around, and ran on to the landing. Feeling blindly in front of him, he made his way to the top of the stairs; he looked down the dark stairs into the hall, seeing a host of shadows curve in and out of the corners, hearing their sinuous voices, imagining the pits of their eyes and their lean arms. But they would be little and secret and bloodless, not cased in invisible armour but wound around with cloths as thin as a web; they would whisper as he walked, touch him on the shoulder, and say S in his ear. He went down the stairs; not a shadow moved in the hall, the corners were empty. He put out his hand and patted the darkness, thinking to feel some dry and velvet head creep under the fingers and edge, like a mist, into the nails. But there was nothing. He opened the front door, and the shadows swept into the garden.

Once on the path, his fears left him. The moon had lain down on the unweeded beds, and her frosts were spread on the grass. At last he came to the illuminated tree at the long gravel end, older even than the marvel of light, with the woodlice asleep under the bark, with the boughs standing out from the body like the frozen arms of a woman. The child touched the tree; it bent as to his touch. He

saw a star, brighter than any in the sky, burn steadily above
the first birds' tower, and shine on nowhere but on the
leafless boughs and the trunk and the travelling roots.

The child had not doubted the tree.   He said his prayers
to it, with knees bent on the blackened twigs the night wind
fetched to the ground.   Then, trembling with love and
cold, he ran back over the lawns towards the house.

There was an idiot to the east of the county who walked
the land like a beggar.   Now at a farmhouse and now at a
widow's cottage he begged for his bread.   A parson gave
him a suit, and it lopped round his hungry ribs and shoulders
and waved in the wind as he shambled over the fields.
But his eyes were so wide and his neck so clear of the
country dirt that no one refused him what he asked.   And
asking for water, he was given milk.

'Where do you come from?'

'From the east,' he said.

So they knew he was an idiot, and gave him a meal to
clean the yards.

As he bent with a rake over the dung and the trodden
grain, he heard a voice rise in his heart.   He put his hand
into the cattle's hay, caught a mouse, rubbed his hand over
its muzzle, and let it go away.

All day the thought of the tree was with the child; all
night it stood up in his dreams as the star stood above its
plot.   One morning towards the middle of December,
when the wind from the farthest hills was rushing around
the house, and the snow of the dark hours had not dissolved
from lawns and roofs, he ran to the gardener's shed.   The
gardener was repairing a rake he had found broken.   Without a word, the child sat on a seedbox at his feet, and
watched him tie the teeth, and knew that the wire would

not keep them together. He looked at the gardener's boots, wet with snow, at the patched knees of his trousers, at the undone buttons of his coat, and the folds of his belly under the patched flannel shirt. He looked at his hands as they busied themselves over the golden knots of wire; they were hard, brown hands, with the stains of the soil under the broken nails and the stains of tobacco on the tips of the fingers. Now the lines of the gardener's face were set in determination as time upon time he knotted the iron teeth only to feel them shake insecurely from the handle. The child was frightened of the strength and uncleanliness of the old man; but, looking at the long, thick beard, unstained and white as fleece, he soon became reassured. The beard was the beard of an apostle.

'I prayed to the tree,' said the child.

'Always pray to a tree,' said the gardener, thinking of Calvary and Eden.

'I pray to the tree every night.'

'Pray to a tree.'

The wire slid over the teeth.

'I pray to that tree.'

The wire snapped.

The child was pointing over the glasshouse flowers to the tree that, alone of all the trees in the garden, had no sign of snow.

'An elder,' said the gardener, but the child stood up from his box and shouted so loud that the unmended rake fell with a clatter on the floor.

'The first tree. The first tree you told me of. In the beginning was the tree, you said. I heard you,' the child shouted.

'The elder is as good as another,' said the gardener, lowering his voice to humour the child.

'The first tree of all,' said the child in a whisper.

Reassured again by the gardener's voice, he smiled through the window at the tree, and again the wire crept over the broken rake.

'God grows in strange trees,' said the old man. 'His trees come to rest in strange places.'

As he unfolded the story of the twelve stages of the cross, the tree waved its boughs to the child. An apostle's voice rose out of the tarred lungs.

So they hoisted him up on a tree, and drove nails through his belly and his feet.

There was the blood of the noon sun on the trunk of the elder, staining the bark.

.   .   .   .

The idiot stood on the Jarvis hills, looking down into the immaculate valley from whose waters and grasses the mists of morning rose and were lost. He saw the dew dissolving, the cattle staring into the stream, and the dark clouds flying away at the rumour of the sun. The sun turned at the edges of the thin and watery sky like a sweet in a glass of water. He was hungry for light as the first and almost invisible rain fell on his lips; he plucked at the grass, and, tasting it, felt it lie green on his tongue. So there was light in his mouth, and light was a sound at his ears, and the whole dominion of light in the valley that had such a curious name. He had known of the Jarvis hills; their shapes rose over the slopes of the county to be seen for miles around, but no one had told him of the valley lying under the hills. Bethlehem, said the idiot to the valley, turning over the sounds of the word and giving it all the glory of the Welsh morning. He brothered the world around him, sipped at the air, as a child newly born sips and brothers the light. The life of the Jarvis valley, steaming up from the body of the grass and the

trees and the long hand of the stream, lent him a new blood.
Night had emptied the idiot's veins, and dawn in the valley
filled them again.

'Bethlehem,' said the idiot to the valley.

The gardener had no present to give the child, so he
took out a key from his pocket and said: 'This is the key
to the tower.   On Christmas Eve I will unlock the door
for you.'

Before it was dark, he and the child climbed the stairs
to the tower, the key turned in the lock, and the door, like
the lid of a secret box, opened and let them in.   The room
was empty.   'Where are the secrets?' asked the child,
staring up at the matted rafters and into the spider's corners
and along the leaden panes of the window.

'It is enough that I have given you the key,' said the
gardener, who believed the key of the universe to be hidden
in his pocket along with the feathers of birds and the seeds of
flowers.

The child began to cry because there were no secrets.
Over and over again he explored the empty room, kicking
up the dust to look for a colourless trap-door, tapping the
unpanelled walls for the hollow voice of a room beyond the
tower.   He brushed the webs from the window, and looked
out through the dust into the snowing Christmas Eve.   A
world of hills stretched far away into the measured sky, and
the tops of hills he had never seen climbed up to meet the
falling flakes.   Woods and rocks, wide seas of barren land,
and a new tide of mountain sky sweeping through the black
beeches, lay before him.   To the east were the outlines of
nameless hill creatures and a den of trees.

'Who are they?   Who are they?'

'They are the Jarvis hills,' said the gardener, 'which have
been from the beginning.'

He took the child by the hand and led him away from the window. The key turned in the lock.

That night the child slept well; there was power in snow and darkness; there was unalterable music in the silence of the stars; there was a silence in the hurrying wind. And Bethlehem had been nearer than he expected.

. . . .

On Christmas morning the idiot walked into the garden. His hair was wet and his flaked and ragged shoes were thick with the dirt of the fields. Tired with the long journey from the Jarvis hills, and weak for the want of food, he sat down under the elder-tree where the gardener had rolled a log. Clasping his hands in front of him, he saw the desolation of the flower-beds and the weeds that grew in profusion on the edges of the paths. The tower stood up like a tree of stone and glass over the red eaves. He pulled his coat-collar round his neck as a fresh wind sprang up and struck the tree; he looked down at his hands and saw that they were praying. Then a fear of the garden came over him, the shrubs were his enemies, and the trees that made an avenue down to the gate lifted their arms in horror. The place was too high, peering down on to the tall hills; the place was too low, shivering up at the plumed shoulders of a new mountain. Here the wind was too wild, fuming about the silence, raising a Jewish voice out of the elder boughs; here the silence beat like a human heart. And as he sat under the cruel hills, he heard a voice that was in him cry out: 'Why did you bring me here?'

He could not tell why he had come; they had told him to come and had guided him, but he did not know who they were. The voice of a people rose out of the garden beds, and rain swooped down from heaven.

'Let me be,' said the idiot, and made a little gesture against the sky.   There is rain on my face, there is wind on my cheeks.   He brothered the rain.

So the child found him under the shelter of the tree, bearing the torture of the weather with a divine patience, letting his long hair blow where it would, with his mouth set in a sad smile.

Who was this stranger?   He had fires in his eyes, the flesh of his neck under the gathered coat was bare.   Yet he smiled as he sat in his rags under a tree on Christmas Day.

'Where do you come from?' asked the child.

'From the east,' answered the idiot.

The gardener had not lied, and the secret of the tower was true; this dark and shabby tree, that glistened only in the night, was the first tree of all.

But he asked again:

'Where do you come from?'

'From the Jarvis hills.'

'Stand up against the tree.'

The idiot, still smiling, stood up with his back to the elder.

'Put out your arms like this.'

The idiot put out his arms.

The child ran as fast as he could to the gardener's shed, and, returning over the sodden lawns, saw that the idiot had not moved but stood, straight and smiling, with his back to the tree and his arms stretched out.

'Let me tie your hands.'

The idiot felt the wire that had not mended the rake close round his wrists.   It cut into the flesh, and the blood from the cuts fell shining on to the tree.

'Brother,' he said.   He saw that the child held silver nails in the palm of his hand.

The Map of Love

'Here dwell,' said Sam Rib, the 'two-backed beasts.'
He pointed to his map of Love, a square of seas and islands
and strange continents with a forest of darkness at each
extremity. The two-backed island, on the line of the
equator, went in like the skin of lupus to his touch, and the
blood sea surrounding found a new motion in its waters.
Here seed, up the tide, broke on the boiling coasts; the
sand grains multiplied; the seasons passed; summer, in a
father's heat, went down to the autumn and the first pricks
of winter, leaving the island shaping the four contrary winds
out of its hollows.

'Here,' said Sam Rib, digging his fingers in the hills of a
little island, 'dwell the first beasts of love.' And here the
get of the first loves mixed, as he knew, with the grasses
that oiled their green upgoings, with their own wind and
sap nurtured the first rasp of love that never, until spring
came, found the nerves' answer in the fellowing blades.

Beth Rib and Reuben marked the green sea around the
island. It ran through the landcracks like a boy through his
first caves. Under the sea they marked the channels,
painted in skeleton, that linked the first beasts' island with
the boggy lands. For shame of the half-liquid plants
sprouting from the bog, the pen-drawn poisons seething in
the grass, and the copulation in the second mud, the children
blushed.

'Here,' said Sam Rib, 'two weathers move.' He traced
with his finger the lightly drawn triangles of two winds,
and the mouths of two cornered cherubs. The weathers

moved in one direction. Singly they crawled over the abominations of the swamp, content in the shadow of their own rains and snowings, in the noise of their own sighs, and the pleasures of their own green achings. The weathers, like a girl and a boy, moved through the tossing world, the sea storm dragging under them, the clouds divided in many rages of movement as they stared on the raw wall of wind.

'Return, synthetic prodigals, to thy father's laboratory,' declaimed Sam Rib, 'and the fatted calf in a test-tube.' He indicated the shift of locations, the pen lines of the separate weathers travelling over the deep sea and the second split between the lovers' worlds. The cherubs blew harder; wind of the two tossing weathers and the sprays of the cohering sea drove on and on; on the single strand of two coupled countries, the weathers stood. Two naked towers on the two-loves-in-a-grain of the million sands, they mixed, so the map arrows said, into a single strength. But the arrows of ink shot them back; two weakened towers, wet with love, they trembled at the terror of their first mixing, and two pale shadows blew over the land.

Beth Rib and Reuben scaled the hill that cast an eye of stone on the striped valley; hand-in-hand they ran down the hill, singing as they went, and took off their gaiters at the wet grass of the first of the twenty fields. There was a spirit in the valley that would roll on when all the hills and trees, all the rocks and streams, had been buried under the West death. Here was the first field wherein mad Jarvis, a hundred years before, had sown his seed in the belly of a bald-headed girl who had wandered out of a distant county and lain with him in the pains of love.

Here was the fourth field, a place of wonder, where the dead might spin all drunken-legged out of the dry graves, or the fallen angels battle upon the waters of the streams.

Planted deeper in the soil of the valley than the blind roots could burrow after their mates, the spirit of the fourth field rose out of darkness, drawing the deep and the dark from the hearts of all who trod the valley a score or more miles from the borders of the mountainous county.

In the tenth and the central field Beth Rib and Reuben knocked at the doors of the bungalows, asking the location of the first island surrounded by loving hills. They knocked at the back door and received a ghostly admonishment.

Barefooted and hand-in-hand, they ran through the ten remaining fields to the edge of the Idris water where the wind smelt of seaweed and the valley spirit was set with sea rain. But night came down, hand on thigh, and shapes in the further stretches of the now misty river drew a new shape close to them. An island shape walled round with darkness a half-mile up river. Stealthily Beth Rib and Reuben tiptoed to the lapping water. They saw the shape grow, unlocked their fingers, took off their summer clothes, and, naked, raced into the river.

'Up river, up river,' she whispered.

'Up river,' he said.

They floated down river as a current tugged at their legs, but they fought off the current and swam towards the still growing island. Then mud rose from the bed of the river and sucked at Beth's feet.

'Down river, down river,' she called, and struggled from the mud.

Reuben, weed-bound, fought with the grey heads that fought his hands, and followed her back to the brink of the sea-going valley.

But, as Beth swam, the water tickled her; the water pressed on her side.

'My love,' cried Reuben, excited by the tickling water and the hands of the weeds.

And, as they stood naked on the twentieth field, 'My love,' she whispered.

First fear shot them back. Wet as they were, they pulled their clothes on them.

'Over the fields,' she said.

Over the fields, in the direction of the hills and the hill-home of Sam Rib, like weakened towers the children ran, no longer linked, bewildered by the mud and blushing at the first tickle of the misty island water.

'Here dwell,' said Sam Rib, 'the first beasts of love.' In the cool of a new morning the children listened, too frightened to touch hands. He touched again the sagging hill above the island, and pointed the progression of the skeleton channels linking mud with mud, green sea with darker, and all love-hills and islands into one territory. 'Here the grass mates, the green mates, the grains,' said Sam Rib, 'and the dividing waters mate and are mated. The sun with the grass and the green, sand with water, and water with the green grass, these mate and are mated for the bearing and fostering of the globe.' Sam Rib had mated with a green woman, as Great-Uncle Jarvis with his bald girl; he had mated with a womanly water for the bearing and the fostering of the child who blushed by him. He marked how the boggy lands lay so near the first beast doubling a back, the round of doubled beasts under as high a hill as Great-Uncle's hill that had frowned last night and wrapped itself in stones. Great-Uncle's hill had cut the children's feet, for the daps and the gaiters were lost for ever in the grass of the first field.

Thinking of the hill, Beth Rib and Reuben sat quiet. They heard Sam say that the hill of the first island grew soft as wool for the descent, or smooth as ice for tobogganing. They remembered the tame descent last night.

'Tame hill,' said Sam Rib, grows wild for the ascending.

Lining the adolescents' hill was a white route of stone and ice marked with the sliding foot or sledge of the children going down; another route, at the foot, climbed upwards in a line of red stone and blood marked with the cracking prints of the ascending children. The descent was soft as wool. Fail on the first island, and the ascending hill wraps itself in a sharp thing of stones.

Beth Rib and Reuben, never forgetful of the humpbacked boulders and the flints in the grass, turned to each other for the first time that day. Sam Rib had made her and would mould him, would make and mould the boy and girl together into a double climber that sought the island and melted there into a single strength. He told them again of the mud, but did not frighten them. And the grey heads of the weeds were broken, never to swell again in the hands of the swimmer. The day of ascending was over; the first descent remained, a hill on the map of love, two branches of stone and olive in the children's hands.

Synthetic prodigals returned that night to the room of the hill, through caves and chambers running to the roof, discerning the roof of stars, and happy in their locked hands. There lay the striped valley before them, and the grass of the twenty fields fed the cattle; the night cattle moved by the hedges or lapped at warm Idris water. Beth Rib and Reuben ran down the hill, and the tender stones lay still under their feet; faster, they ran down the Jarvis flank, the wind at their hair, smells of the sea blown to their quivering nostrils from the north and the south where there was no sea; and, slowing their speed, they reached the first field and the rim of the valley to find their gaiters placed neatly in a cow-cloven spot in the grass.

They buttoned on their gaiters, and ran through the falling blades.

'Here is the first field,' said Beth Rib to Reuben.

The children stopped, the moonlight night went on, a voice spoke from the hedge darkness.

Said the voice: 'You are the children of love.'

'Where are you?'

'I am Jarvis.'

'Who are you?'

'Here, my dears, here in the hedge with a wise woman.'

But the children ran away from the voice in the hedge.

'Here in the second field.'

They stopped for breath, and a weasel, making his noise, ran over their feet.

'Hold harder.'

'I'll hold you harder.'

Said a voice: 'Hold hard, the children of love.'

'Where are you?'

'I am Jarvis.'

'Who are you?'

'Here, here, lying with a virgin from Dolgelley.'

In the third field the man of Jarvis lay loving a green girl, and, as he called them the children of love, lay loving her ghost and the smell of buttermilk on her breath.   He loved a cripple in the fourth field, for the twist in her limbs made loving longer, and he cursed the straight children who found him with a straight-limbed lover in the fifth field marking the quarter.

A girl from Tiger Bay held Jarvis close, and her lips marked a red, cracked heart upon his throat; this was the sixth and the weather-tracked field where, turning from the maul of her hands, he saw their innocence, two flowers wagging in a sow's ear.   'My rose,' said Jarvis, but the seventh love smelt in his hands, his fingering hands that held Glamorgan's canker under the eighth hedge.   From the Convent of Bethel's Heart, a holy woman served him the ninth time.

And the children in the central field cried as ten voices came up, came up, came down from the ten spaces of the half-night and the hedging world.

It was full night when they answered, when the voices of one voice compassionately answered the two-voiced question ringing on the strokes of the upward, upward, and the downward air.

'We,' said they, 'are Jarvis, Jarvis under the hedge, in the arms of a woman, a green woman, a woman bald as a badger, on a nun's thigh.'

They counted the numbers of their loves before the children's ears. Beth Rib and Reuben heard the ten oracles, and shyly they surrendered. Over the remaining fields, to the whispers of the last ten lovers, to the voice of ageing Jarvis, grey-haired in the final shadows, they sped to Idris. The island shone, the water babbled, there was a gesture of the limbs in each wind's stroke denting the flat river. He took off her summer clothes, and she shaped her arms like a swan. The bare boy stood at her shoulder; and she turned and saw him dive into the ripples in her wake. Behind them her fathers' voices slipped out of sound.

'Up river,' called Beth, 'up river.'

'Up river,' he answered.

Only the warm, mapped waters ran that night over the edges of the first beasts' island white in a new moon.

The Mouse and the Woman

In the eaves of the lunatic asylum were birds who whistled the coming in of spring. A madman, howling like a dog from the top room, could not disturb them, and their tunes did not stop when he thrust his hands through the bars of the window near their nests and clawed the sky. A fresh smell blew with the winds around the white building and its grounds. The asylum trees waved green hands over the wall to the world outside.

In the gardens the patients sat and looked up at the sun or upon the flowers or upon nothing, or walked sedately along the paths, hearing the gravel crunch beneath their feet with a hard, sensible sound. Children in print dresses might be expected to play, not noisily, upon the lawns. The building too had a sweet expression, as though it knew only the kind things of life and the polite emotions. In a middle room sat a child who had cut off his double thumb with a scissors.

A little way off the main path leading from house to gate, a girl, lifting her arms, beckoned to the birds. She enticed the sparrows with little movements of her fingers, but to no avail. 'It must be spring,' she said. The sparrows sang exultantly, and then stopped.

The howling in the top room began again. The madman's face was pressed close to the bars of the window. Opening his mouth wide, he bayed up at the sun, listening to the inflections of his voice with a remorseless concentration.

With his unseeing eyes fixed on the green garden, he heard the revolution of the years as they moved softly back. Now there was no garden. Under the sun the iron bars melted. Like a flower, a new room pulsed and opened.

Waking up when it was still dark, he turned the dream over and over on the tip of his brain until each little symbol became heavy with a separate meaning. But there were symbols he could not remember, they came and went so quickly among the rattle of leaves, the gestures of women's hands spelling on the sky, the falling of rain and the humming wind. He remembered the oval of her face and the colour of her eyes. He remembered the pitch of her voice, though not what she said. She moved again wearily up and down the same ruler of turf. What she said fell with the leaves, and spoke in the wind whose brother rattled the panes like an old man.

There had been seven women, in a mad play by a Greek, each with the same face, crowned by the same hoop of mad, black hair. One by one they trod the ruler of turf, then vanished. They turned the same face to him, intolerably weary with the same suffering.

The dream had changed. Where the women were was an avenue of trees. And the trees leant forward and interlaced their hands, turning into a black forest. He had seen himself, absurd in his nakedness, walk into the depths. Stepping on a dead twig, he was bitten.

Then there was her face again. There was nothing in his dream but her tired face. And the changes of the details of the dream and the celestial changes, the levers of the trees and the toothed twigs, these were the mechanisms of her

delirium.   It was not the sickness of sin that was upon her
face.   Rather it was the sickness of never having sinned and
of never having done well.

He lit the candle on the little deal table by his bedside.
Candle light threw the shadows of the room into confusion,
and raised up the warped men of shadow out of the corners.
For the first time he heard the clock.   He had been deaf
until then to everything except the wind outside the window
and the clean winter sounds of the nightworld.   But now
the steady tick tock tick sounded like the heart of someone
hidden in his room.   He could not hear the night birds
now.   The loud clock drowned their crying, or the wind
was too cold for them and made commotion among their
feathers.   He remembered the dark hair of the woman in
the trees and of the seven women treading the ruler of turf.

He could no longer listen to the speaking of reason.   The
pulse of a new heart beat at his side.   Contentedly he let
the dream dictate its rhythm.   Often he would rise when
the sun had dropped down, and, in the lunatic blackness
under the stars, walk on the hill, feeling the wind finger his
hair and at his nostrils.   The rats and the rabbits on his
towering hill came out in the dark, and the shadows con-
soled them for the light of the harsh sun.   The dark woman,
too, had risen out of darkness, pulling down the stars in
their hundreds and showing him a mystery that hung and
shone higher in the night of the sky than all the planets
crowding beyond the curtains.

He fell to sleep again and woke in the sun.   As he
dressed, the dog scratched at the door.   He let it in and felt
its wet muzzle in his hand.   The weather was hot for a mid-
winter day.   The little wind there was could not relieve
the sharpness of the heat.   With the opening of the bedroom window, the uneven beams of the sun twisted his
images into the hard lines of light.

He tried not to think of the woman as he ate.   She had risen out of the depths of darkness.   Now she was lost again.   She is drowned, dead, dead.   In the clean glittering of the kitchen, among the white boards, the oleographs of old women, the brass candlesticks, the plates on the shelves, and the sounds of kettle and clock, he was caught between believing in her and denying her.   Now he insisted on the lines of her neck.   The wilderness of her hair rose over the dark surface.   He saw her flesh in the cut bread; her blood, still flowing through the channels of her mysterious body, in the spring water.

But another voice told him that she was dead.   She was a woman in a mad story.   He forced himself to hear the voice telling that she was dead.   Dead, alive, drowned, raised up.   The two voices shouted across his brain.   He could not bear to think that the last spark in her had been put out.   She is alive, alive, cried the two voices together.

As he tidied the sheets on his bed, he saw a block of paper, and sat down at the table with a pencil poised in his hand. A hawk flew over the hill.   Seagulls, on spread, unmoving wings, cried past the window.   A mother rat, in a hole in the hillside near the holes of rabbits, suckled its young as the sun climbed higher in the clouds.

He put the pencil down.

3

One winter morning, after the last crowing of the cock, in the walks of his garden, had died to nothing, she who for so long had dwelt with him appeared in all the wonder of her youth.   She had cried to be set free, and to walk in his dreams no longer.   Had she not been in the beginning, there would have been no beginning.   She had moved in his belly when he was a boy, and stirred in his boy's loins. He at last gave birth to her who had been with him from the beginning. And with him dwelt a dog, a mouse, and a dark woman.

4

It is not a little thing, he thought, this writing that lies before me. It is the telling of a creation. It is the story of birth. Out of him had come another. A being had been born, not out of the womb, but out of the soul and the spinning head. He had come to the cottage on the hill that the being within him might ripen and be born away from the eyes of men. He understood what the wind that took up the woman's cry had cried in his last dream. 'Let me be born,' it had cried. He had given a woman being. His flesh would be upon her, and the life that he had given her would make her walk, talk, and sing. And he knew, too, that it was upon the block of paper she was made absolute. There was an oracle in the lead of the pencil.

In the kitchen he cleaned up after his meal. When the last plate had been washed, he looked around the room. In the corner near the door was a hole no bigger than a half-crown. He found a tiny square of tin and nailed it over the hole, making sure that nothing could go in or come out. Then he donned his coat and walked out on to the hill and down towards the sea.

Broken water leapt up from the inrushing tide and fell into the crevices of the rocks, making innumerable pools. He climbed down to the half-circle of beach, and the clusters of shells did not break when his foot fell on them. Feeling his heart knock at his side, he turned to where the greater rocks climbed perilously up to the grass. There, at the

foot, the oval of her face towards him, she stood and smiled.
The spray brushed her naked body, and the creams of the
sea ran unheeded over her feet. She lifted her hand. He
crossed to her.

5

In the cool of the evening they walked in the garden
behind the cottage. She had lost none of her beauty with
the covering up of her nakedness. With slippers on her
feet she stepped as gracefully as when her feet were bare.
There was a dignity in the poise of her head, and her voice
was clear as a bell. Walking by her side along the narrow
path, he heard no discord in the crying together of the gulls.
She pointed out bird and bush with her finger, illuminating
a new loveliness in the wings and leaves, in the sour
churning of water over pebbles, and a new life along the
dead branches of the trees.

'It is quiet here,' she said as they stood looking out to
sea and the dark coming over the land. 'Is it always as
quiet?'

'Not when the storms come in with the tide,' he said.
'Boys play behind the hill, lovers go down to the shore.'

Late evening turned to night so suddenly that, where she
stood, stood a shadow under the moon. He took its hand,
and they ran together to the cottage.

'It was lonely for you before I came,' she said.

As a cinder hissed into the grate, he moved back in his
chair, made a startled gesture with his hand.

'How quickly you become frightened,' she said, 'I am
frightened of nothing.'

But she thought over her words and spoke again, this
time in a low voice.

'One day I may have no limbs to walk with, no hands to touch with.   No heart under my breast.'

'Look at the million stars,' he said.   'They make some pattern on the sky.   It is a pattern of letters spelling a word. One night I shall look up and read the word.'

But she kissed him and calmed his fears.

6

The madman remembered the inflections of her voice, heard, again, her frock rustling, and saw the terrible curve of her breast.   His own breathing thundered in his ears. The girl on the bench beckoned to the sparrows.   Some-where a child purred, stroking the black columns of a wooden horse that neighed and then lay down.

7

They slept together on the first night, side by side in the dark, their arms around one another.   The shadows in the corner were trimmed and shapely in her presence, losing their old deformity.   And the stars looked in upon them and shone in their eyes.

'To-morrow you must tell me what you dream,' he said.

'It will be what I have always dreamed,' she said. 'Walking on a little length of grass, up and down, up and down, till my feet bleed.   Seven images of me walking up and down.'

'It is what I dream.   Seven is a number in magic.'

'Magic?' she said.

'A woman makes a wax man, puts a pin in its chest; and

the man dies. Someone has a little devil, tells it what to do. A girl dies, you see her walk. A woman turns into a hill.'

She let her head rest on his shoulder, and fell to sleep.

He kissed her mouth, and passed his hand through her hair.

She was asleep, but he did not sleep. Wide awake, he stared into darkness. Now he was drowned in terror, and the sucking waters closed over his skull.

'I, I have a devil,' he said.

She stirred at the noise of his voice, and then again her head was motionless and her body straight along the curves of the cool bed.

'I have a devil, but I do not tell it what to do. It lifts my hand. I write. The words spring into life. She, then, is a woman of the devil.'

She made a contented sound, nestled ever nearer to him. Her breath was warm on his neck, and her foot lay on his like a mouse. He saw that she was beautiful in her sleep. Her beauty could not have sprouted out of evil. God, whom he had searched for in his loneliness, had formed her for his mate as Eve for Adam out of Adam's rib.

He kissed her again, and saw her smile as she slept.

'God at my side,' he said.

8

He had not slept with Rachel and woken with Leah. There was the pallor of dawn on her cheeks. He touched them lightly with a finger-nail. She did not stir.

But there had been no woman in his dream. Not even a thread of woman's hair had dangled from the sky. God had come down in a cloud and the cloud had changed to a snakes' nest. Foul hissing of snakes had suggested the sound of water, and he had been drowned. Down and down he had fallen, under green shiftings and the bubbles that fishes blew from their mouths, down and down on to the bony floors of the sea.

Then against a white curtain people had moved and moved to no purpose but to speak mad things.

'What did you find under the tree?'

'I found an airman.'

'No, no, under the other tree?'

'I found a bottle of foetus.'

'No, no, under the other tree?'

'I found a mouse-trap.'

He had been invisible. There had been nothing but his voice. He had flown across back gardens, and his voice, caught in a tangle of wireless aerials, had bled as though it were a thing of substance. Men in deck-chairs were listening to the loud-speakers speaking:

'What did you find under the tree?'

'I found a wax man.'

'No, no, under the other tree?'

He could remember little else except the odds and ends of sentences, the movement of a turning shoulder, the sudden flight or drop of syllables. But slowly the whole meaning edged into his brain. He could translate every symbol of his dreams, and he lifted the pencil so that they might stand hard and clear upon the paper. But the words would not come. He thought he heard the scratching of velvet paws behind a panel. But when he sat still and listened close, there was no sound.

She opened her eyes.

'What are you doing?' she said.

He put down the paper, and kissed her before they rose to dress.

'What did you dream last night?' he asked her, when they had eaten.

'Nothing. I slept, that is all. What did you dream?'

'Nothing,' he said.

9

There was creation screaming in the steam of the kettle, in the light making mouths on the china and the floor she swept as a child sweeps the floor of a doll's house. There was nothing to see in her but the ebb and flood of creation, only the transcendent sweep of being and living in the careless fold of flesh from shoulder-bone to elbow. He could not tell, after the horror he had found in the translating symbols, why the sea should point to the fruitful and unfailing stars with the edge of each wave, and an image of fruition disturb the moon in its dead course.

She moulded his images that evening. She lent light, and the lamp was dim beside her who had the oil of life glistening in every pore of her hand.

And now in the garden they remembered how they had walked in the garden for the first time.

'You were lonely before I came.'

'How quickly you become frightened.'

She had lost none of her beauty with the covering up of her nakedness. Though he had slept at her side, he had been content to know the surface of her. Now he stripped her of her clothes and laid her on a bed of grass.

10

The mouse had waited for this consummation. Wrinkling

its eyes, it crept stealthily along the tunnel, littered with scraps of half-eaten paper, behind the kitchen wall. Stealthily, on tiny, padded paws, it felt its way through darkness, its nails scraping on the wood. Stealthily, it worked its way between the walls, screamed at the blind light through the chinks, and filed through the square of tin. Moonlight dropped slowly into the space where the mouse, working its destruction, inched into light. The last barrier fell away. And on the clean stones of the kitchen floor the mouse stood still.

II

That night he told of the love in the garden of Eden.

'A garden was planted eastward, and Adam lived in it. Eve was made for him, out of him, bone of his bones, flesh of his flesh. They were as naked as you upon the seashore, but Eve could not have been as beautiful. They ate with the devil, and saw that they were naked, and covered up their nakedness. In their good bodies they saw evil for the first time.'

'Then you saw evil in me,' she said, 'when I was naked. I would as soon be naked as be clothed. Why did you cover up my nakedness?'

'It was not good to look upon,' he said.

'But it was beautiful. You yourself said that it was beautiful,' she said.

'It was not good to look upon.'

'You said the body of Eve was good. And yet you say I was not good to look upon. Why did you cover up my nakedness?'

'It was not good to look upon.'

12

'Welcome,' said the devil to the madman. 'Cast your eyes upon me. I grow and grow. See how I multiply. See my sad, Grecian stare. And the longing to be born in my dark eyes. Oh, that was the best joke of all.'

'I am an asylum boy tearing the wings of birds. Remember the lions that were crucified. Who knows that it was not I who opened the door of the tomb for Christ to struggle out?'

But the madman had heard that welcome time after time. Ever since the evening of the second day after their love in the garden, when he had told her that her nakedness was not good to look upon, he had heard the welcome ring out in the sliding rain, and seen the welcome words burnt into the sea. He had known at the ringing of the first syllable in his ears that nothing on the earth could save him, and that the mouse would come out.

But the mouse had come out already.

The madman cried down at the beckoning girl to whom, now, a host of birds edged closer on a bough.

13

'Why did you cover up my nakedness?'

'It was not good to look upon.'

'Why, then, No, no, under the other tree?'

'It was not good, I found a wax cross.'

As she had questioned him, not harshly, but with bewilderment, that he whom she loved should find her nakedness unclean, he heard the broken pieces of the old dirge break into her questioning.

'Why, then,' she said, 'No, no, under the other tree?'

He heard himself reply, 'It was not good, I found a talking thorn.'

Real things kept changing place with unreal, and, as a bird burst into song, he heard the springs rattle far back in its throat.

She left him with a smile that still poised over a question, and, crossing the strip of hill, vanished into the half-dark where the cottage stood like another woman. But she returned ten times, in ten different shapes. She breathed at his ear, passed the back of her hand over his dry mouth, and lit the lamp in the cottage room more than a mile away.

It grew darker as he stared at the stars. Wind cut through the new night. Very suddenly a bird screamed over the trees, and an owl, hungry for mice, hooted in the mile-away wood.

There was contradiction in heartbeat and green Sirius, an eye in the east. He put his hand to his eyes, hiding the star, and walked slowly towards the lamp burning far away in the cottage. And all the elements come together, of wind and sea and fire, of love and the passing of love, closed in a circle around him.

She was not sitting by the fire, as he had expected her to be, smiling upon the folds of her dress. He called her name at the foot of the stairs. He looked into the empty bedroom, and called her name in the garden. But she had gone, and all the mystery of her presence had left the cottage. And the shadows that he thought had departed when she had come crowded the corners, muttering in women's voices among themselves. He turned down the wick in the lamp. As he climbed upstairs, he heard the corner voices become louder and louder until the whole cottage reverberated with them, and the wind could not be heard.

14

With tears in his cheeks and with a hard pain in his heart, he fell to sleep, coming at last to where his father sat in an alcove carved in a cloud.

'Father,' he said, 'I have been walking over the world, looking for a thing worthy to love, but I drove it away and go now from place to place, moaning my hideousness, hearing my own voice in the voices of the corncrakes and the frogs, seeing my own face in the riddled faces of the beasts.'

He held out his arms, waiting for words to fall from that old mouth hidden under a white beard frozen with tears. He implored the old man to speak.

'Speak to me, your son. Remember how we read the classic books together on the terraces. Or on an Irish harp you would pluck tunes until the geese, like the seven geese of the Wandering Jew, rose squawking into the air. Father, speak to me, your only son, a prodigal out of the herbaceous spaces of small towns, out of the smells and sounds of the city, out of the thorny desert and the deep sea. You are a wise old man.'

He implored the old man to speak, but, coming closer to him and staring into his face, he saw the stains of death upon mouth and eyes and a nest of mice in the tangle of the frozen beard.

It was weak to fly, but he flew. And it was a weakness of the blood to be invisible, but he was invisible. He reasoned and dreamed unreasonably at the same time, knowing his weakness and the lunacy of flying but having no strength to conquer it. He flew like a bird over the fields, but soon the bird's body vanished, and he was a flying voice. An open window beckoned him by the waving of its blinds, as a scarecrow beckons a wise bird by its ragged waving, and into the open window he flew, alighting on a bed near a sleeping girl.

'Awake, girl,' he said. 'I am your lover come in the night.'

She awoke at his voice.

'Who called me?'

'I called you.'

'Where are you?'

'I am upon the pillow by your head, speaking into your ear.'

'Who are you?'

'I am a voice.'

'Stop calling into my ear, then, and hop into my hand so that I may touch you and tickle you. Hop into my hand, voice.'

He lay still and warm in her palm.

'Where are you?'

'I am in your hand.'

'Which hand?'

'The hand on your breast, left hand. Do not make a fist or you will crush me. Can you not feel me warm in your hand? I am close to the roots of your fingers.'

'Talk to me.'

'I had a body, but was always a voice. As I truly am, I come to you in the night, a voice on your pillow.'

'I know what you are. You are the still, small voice I must not listen to. I have been told not to listen to that still, small voice that speaks in the night. It is wicked to listen. You must not come here again. You must go away.'

'But I am your lover.'

'I must not listen,' said the girl, and suddenly clenched her hand.

15

He could go into the garden, regardless of rain, and bury his face in the wet earth. With his ears pressed close to the earth, he would hear the great heart, under soil and grass, strain before breaking. In dreams he would say to some figure, 'Lift me up. I am only ten pounds now. I am lighter. Six pounds. Two pounds. My spine shows through my breast.' The secret of that alchemy that had turned a little revolution of the unsteady senses into a golden moment was lost as a key is lost in undergrowth. A secret was confused among the night, and the confusion of the last madness before the grave would come down like an animal on the brain.

He wrote upon the block of paper, not knowing what he wrote, and dreading the words that looked up at him at last and could not be forgotten.

16

And this is all there was to it: a woman had been born, not out of the womb, but out of the soul and the spinning head. And he who had borne her out of darkness loved his creation, and she loved him. But this is all there was to it: a miracle befell a man. He fell in love with it, but could not keep it, and the miracle passed. And with him dwelt a dog, a mouse, and a dark woman. The woman went away, and the dog died.

17

He buried the dog at the end of the garden. 'Rest in peace,' he told the dead dog. But the grave was not deep enough and there were rats in the under-hanging of the bank who bit through the sack shroud.

18

Upon town pavements he saw the woman step loose, her breasts firm under a coat on which the single hairs from old men's heads lay white on black. Her life, he knew, was only a life of days. Her spring had passed with him. After the summer and the autumn, unhallowed time between full life and death, there would be winter corrugating charm. He who knew the subtleties of every reason, and sensed the four together in every symbol of the earth, would disturb the chronology of the seasons. Winter must not appear.

19

Consider now the old effigy of time, his long beard whitened by an Egyptian sun, his bare feet watered by the Sargasso sea. Watch me belabour the old fellow. I have stopped his heart. It split like a chamber pot. No, this is no rain falling. This is the wet out of the cracked heart.

Parhelion and sun shine in the same sky with the broken moon. Dizzy with the chasing of moon by sun, and by the twinkling of so many stars, I run upstairs to read again of the love of some man for a woman. I tumble down to see the half-crown hole in the kitchen wall stabbed open, and the prints of a mouse's pads on the floor.

Consider now the old effigies of the seasons.   Break up the rhythm of the old figures' moving, the spring trot, summer canter, sad stride of autumn, and winter shuffle. Break, piece by piece, the continuous changing of motion into a spindle-shanked walking.

Consider the sun for whom I know no image but the old image of a shot eye, and the broken moon.

20

Gradually the chaos became less, and the things of the surrounding world were no longer wrought out of their own substance into the shapes of his thoughts.   Some peace fell about him, and again the music of creation was to be heard trembling out of crystal waters, out of the holy sweep of the sky down to the wet edge of the earth where a sea flowed over.   Night came slowly, and the hill rose to the unrisen stars.   He turned over the block of paper and upon the last page wrote in a clear hand:

21

The woman died.

22

There was dignity in such a murder.   And the hero in him rose up in all his holiness and strength.   It was just that he who had brought her forth from darkness should pack her away again.   And it was just that she should die not knowing what hand out of the sky struck upon her and laid her low.

He walked down the hill, his steps slow as in procession, and his lips smiling at the dark sea.   He climbed on to the shore, and, feeling his heart knock at his side, turned to where the greater rocks climbed perilously to the grass. There at the foot, her face towards him, she lay and smiled. Sea-water ran unheeded over her nakedness.   He crossed to her, and touched her cold cheek with his nails.

23

Acquainted with the last grief, he stood at the open window of his room.   And the night was an island in a sea of mystery and meaning.   And the voice out of the night was a voice of acceptance.   And the face of the moon was the face of humility.

He knew the last wonder before the grave and the mystery that bewilders and incorporates the heavens and the earth. He knew that he had failed before the eye of God and the eye of Sirius to hold his miracle.   The woman had shown him that it was wonderful to live.   And now, when at last he knew how wonderful, and how pleasant the blood in the trees, and how deep the well of the clouds, he must close his eyes and die.   He opened his eyes, and looked up at the stars.   There were a million stars spelling the same word. And the word of the stars was written clearly upon the sky.

24

Alone in the kitchen, among the broken chairs and china, stood the mouse that had come out of the hole.   Its paws rested lightly upon the floor painted all over with the grotesque figures of birds and girls. Stealthily, it crept back into the hole. Stealthily, it worked its way between the walls. There was no sound in the kitchen but the sound of the mouse's nails scraping upon wood.

25

In the eaves of the lunatic asylum the birds still whistled, and the madman, pressed close to the bars of the window near their nests, bayed up at the sun.

Upon the bench some distance from the main path, the girl was beckoning to the birds, while on a square of lawn danced three old women, hand in hand, simpering in the wind, to the music of an Italian organ from the world outside.

'Spring is come,' said the warders.

The Dress

They had followed him for two days over the length of the county, but he had lost them at the foot of the hills, and, hidden in a golden bush, had heard them shouting as they stumbled down the valley. Behind a tree on the ridge of the hills he had peeped down on to the fields where they hurried about like dogs, where they poked the hedges with their sticks and set up a faint howling as a mist came suddenly from the spring sky and hid them from his eyes. But the mist was a mother to him, putting a coat around his shoulders where the shirt was torn and the blood dry on his blades. The mist made him warm; he had the food and the drink of the mist on his lips; and he smiled through her mantle like a cat. He worked away from the valleywards side of the hill into the denser trees that might lead him to light and fire and a basin of soup. He thought of the coals that might be hissing in the grate, and of the young mother standing alone. He thought of her hair. Such a nest it would make for his hands. He ran through the trees, and found himself on a narrow road. Which way should he walk: towards or away from the moon? The mist had made a secret of the position of the moon, but, in a corner of the sky, where the mist had fallen apart, he could see the angles of the stars. He walked towards the north where the stars were, mumbling a song with no tune, hearing his feet suck in and out of the spongy earth.

Now there was time to collect his thoughts, but no sooner had he started to set them in order than an owl made a cry in the trees that hung over the road, and he stopped and

78

winked up at her, finding a mutual melancholy in her sounds. Soon she would swoop and fasten on a mouse. He saw her for a moment as she sat screeching on her bough. Then, frightened of her, he hurried on, and had not gone more than a few yards into the darkness when, with a fresh cry, she flew away. Pity the hare, he thought, for the weasel will drink her. The road sloped to the stars, and the trees and the valley and the memory of the guns faded behind.

He heard footsteps. An old man, radiant with rain, stepped out of the mist.

'Good night, sir,' said the old man.

'No night for the son of woman,' said the madman.

The old man whistled, and hurried, half running, in the direction of the roadside trees.

Let the hounds know, the madman chuckled as he climbed up the hill, let the hounds know. And, crafty as a fox, he doubled back to where the misty road branched off three ways. Hell on the stars, he said, and walked towards the dark.

The world was a ball under his feet; it kicked as he ran; it dropped; up came the trees. In the distance a poacher's dog yelled at the trap on its foot, and he heard it and ran the faster, thinking the enemy was on his heels. 'Duck, boys, duck,' he called out, but with the voice of one who might have pointed to a falling star.

Remembering of a sudden that he had not slept since the escape, he left off running. Now the waters of the rain, too tired to strike the earth, broke up as they fell and blew about in the wind like the sandman's grains. If he met sleep, sleep would be a girl. For the last two nights, while walking or running over the empty county, he had dreamed of their meeting. 'Lie down,' she would say, and would give him her dress to lie on, stretching herself out by his side. Even as he had dreamed, and the twigs under his

running feet had made a noise like the rustle of her dress,
the enemy had shouted in the fields. He had run on and on,
leaving sleep farther behind him. Sometimes there was a
sun, a moon, and sometimes under a black sky he had tossed
and thrown the wind before he could be off.

'Where is Jack?' they asked in the gardens of the place
he had left. 'Up on the hills with a butcher's knife,' they
said, smiling. But the knife was gone, thrown at a tree
and quivering there still. There was no heat in his head.
He ran on and on, howling for sleep.

And she, alone in the house, was sewing her new dress.
It was a bright country dress with flowers on the bodice.
Only a few more stitches were needed before it would be
ready to wear. It would lie neat on her shoulders, and two
of the flowers would be growing out of her breasts.

When she walked with her husband on Sunday mornings
over the fields and down into the village, the boys would
smile at her behind their hands, and the shaping of the dress
round her belly would set all the widow women talking.
She slipped into her new dress, and, looking into the mirror
over the fire-place, saw that it was prettier than she had
imagined. It made her face paler and her long hair darker.
She had cut it low.

A dog out in the night lifted its head up and howled.
She turned away hurriedly from her reflection, and pulled
the curtains closer.

Out in the night they were searching for a madman. He
had green eyes, they said, and had married a lady. They
said he had cut off her lips because she smiled at men. They
took him away, but he stole a knife from the kitchen and
slashed his keeper and broke out into the wild valleys.

From afar he saw the light in the house, and stumbled
up to the edge of the garden. He felt, he did not see, the
little fence around it. The rusting wire scraped on his

hands, and the wet, abominable grass crept over his knees. And once he was through the fence, the hosts of the garden came rushing to meet him, the flower-headed, and the bodying frosts. He had torn his fingers while the old wounds were still wet. Like a man of blood he came out of the enemy's darkness on to the steps. He said in a whisper: 'Let them not shoot me.' And he opened the door.

She was in the middle of the room. Her hair had fallen untidily, and three of the buttons at the neck of her dress were undone. What made the dog howl as it did? Frightened of the howling, and thinking of the tales she had heard, she rocked in her chair. What became of the woman? she wondered as she rocked. She could not think of a woman without any lips. What became of women without any lips? she wondered.

The door made no noise. He stepped into the room, trying to smile, and holding out his hands.

'Oh, you've come back,' she said.

Then she turned in her chair and saw him. There was blood even by his green eyes. She put her fingers to her mouth. 'Not shoot,' he said.

But the moving of her arm drew the neck of her dress apart, and he stared in wonder at her wide, white forehead, her frightened eyes and mouth, and down on to the flowers on her dress. With the moving of her arm, her dress danced in the light. She sat before him, covered in flowers. 'Sleep,' said the madman. And, kneeling down, he put his bewildered head upon her lap.

The Orchards

He had dreamed that a hundred orchards on the road to the sea village had broken into flame; and all the windless afternoon tongues of fire shot through the blossom. The birds had flown up as a small red cloud grew suddenly from each branch; but as night came down with the rising of the moon and the swinging-in of the mile-away sea, a wind blew out the fires and the birds returned. He was an apple-farmer in a dream that ended as it began: with the flesh-and-ghost hand of a woman pointing to the trees. She twined the fair and dark tails of her hair together, smiled over the apple-fields to a sister figure who stood in a circular shadow by the walls of the vegetable garden; but the birds flew down on to her sister's shoulders, unafraid of the scarecrow face and the cross-wood nakedness under the rags. He gave the woman a kiss, and she kissed him back. Then the crows came down to her arms as she held him close; the beautiful scarecrow kissed him, pointing to the trees as the fires died.

Marlais awoke that summer morning with his lips still wet from her kiss. This was a story more terrible than the stories of the reverend madmen in the Black Book of Llareggub, for the woman near the orchards, and her sister-stick by the wall, were his scarecrow lovers for ever and ever. What were the sea-village burning orchards and the clouds at the ends of the branches to his love for these bird-provoking women? All the trees of the world might blaze suddenly from the roots to the highest leaves, but he would not sprinkle water on the shortest fiery field. She was his lover, and her sister with birds on her shoulders held him closer than the women of LlanAsia.

Through the top-storey window he saw the pale blue,
cloudless sky over the tangle of roofs and chimneys, and the
promise of a lovely day in the rivers of the sun.   There, in a
chimney's shape, stood his bare, stone boy and the three
blind gossips, blowing fire through their skulls, who huddled
for warmth in all weathers.   What man on a roof had turned
his weathercock's head to stare at the red-and-black girls
over the town and, by his turning, made them stone pillars?
A wind from the world's end had frozen the roof-walkers
when the town was a handful of houses; now a circle of coal
table-hills, where the children played Indians, cast its shadow
on the black lots and the hundred streets; and the stone-
blind gossips cramped together by his bare boy and the brick
virgins under the towering crane-hills.

The sea ran to the left, a dozen valleys away, past the range
of volcanoes and the great stack forests and ten towns in a
hole.   It met the Glamorgan shores where a half-mountain
fell westward out of the clump of villages in a wild wood,
and shook the base of Wales.   But now, thought Marlais,
the sea is slow and cool, full of dolphins; it flows in all
directions from a green centre, lapping the land stones; it
makes the shells speak on the blazing half-mountain sand,
and the lines of time even shall not join the blue sea surface
and the bottomless bed.

He thought of the sea running; when the sun sank, a fire
went in under the liquid caverns.   He remembered, while
he dressed, the hundred fires around the blossoms of the
apple-trees, and the uneasy salt rising of the wind that died
with the last pointing of the beautiful scarecrow's hand.
Water and fire, sea and apple-tree, two sisters and a crowd
of birds, blossomed, pointed, and flew down all that midsummer morning in a top-storey room in the house on a
slope over the black-housed town.

He sharpened his pencil and shut the sky out, shook back

his untidy hair, arranged the papers of a devilish story on his desk, and broke the pencil-point with a too-hard scribble of 'sea' and 'fire' on a clean page. Fire would not set the ruled lines alight, adventure, burning, through the heartless characters, nor water close over the bogy heads and the unwritten words. The story was dead from the devil up; there was a white-hot tree with apples where a frozen tower with owls should have rocked in a wind from Antarctica; there were naked girls, with nipples like berries, on the sand in the sun, where a cold and unholy woman should be wailing by the Kara Sea or the Sea of Azov. The morning was against him. He struggled with his words like a man with the sun, and the sun stood victoriously at high noon over the dead story.

Put a two-coloured ring of two women's hair round the blue world, white and coal-black against the summer-coloured boundaries of sky and grass, four-breasted stems at the poles of the summer sea-ends, eyes in the sea-shells, two fruit-trees out of a coal-hill: poor Marlais's morning, turning to evening, spins before you. Under the eyelids, where the inward night drove backwards, through the skull's base, into the wide, first world on the far-away eye, two love-trees smouldered like sisters. Have an orchard sprout in the night, an enchanted woman with a spine like a railing burn her hand in the leaves, man-on-fire a mile from a sea have a wind put out your heart: Marlais's death in life in the circular going down of the day that had taken no time blows again in the wind for you.

The world was the saddest in the turning world, and the stars in the north, where the shadow of a mock moon spun until a wind put out the shadow, were the ravaged south faces. Only the fork-tree breast of the woman's scarecrow could bear his head like an apple on the white wood where no worm would enter, and her barbed breast alone pierce the worm in the dream under her sweetheart's eyelid. The real round moon shone on the women of LlanAsia and the love-torn virgins of This street.

The word is too much with us. He raised his pencil so that its shadow fell, a tower of wood and lead, on the clean paper; he fingered the pencil tower, the half-moon of his thumb-nail rising and setting behind the leaden spire. The tower fell, down fell the city of words, the walls of a poem, the symmetrical letters. He marked the disintegration of the ciphers as the light failed, the sun drove down into a foreign morning, and the word of the sea rolled over the sun. 'Image, all image,' he cried to the fallen tower as the night came on. 'Whose harp is the sea? Whose burning candle is the sun?' An image of man, he rose to his feet and drew the curtains open. Peace, like a simile, lay over the roofs of the town. 'Image, all image,' cried Marlais, stepping through the window on to the level roofs.

The slates shone around him, in the smoke of the magnified stacks and through the vapours of the hill. Below him, in a world of words, men on their errands moved to no purpose but the escape of time. Brave in his desolation, he scrambled to the edge of the slates, there to stand perilously above the tiny traffic and the lights of the street signals. The toy of the town was at his feet. On went the marzipan cars, changing gear, applying brake, over the nursery carpets into a child's hands. But soon height had him and he swayed, feeling his legs grow weak beneath him and his skull swell like a bladder in the wind. It was the image of an infant city that threw his pulses into confusion. There was dust in his eyes; there were eyes in the grains of dust ascending from the street. Once on the leveller roofs, he touched his left breast. Death was the bright magnets of the streets; the wind pulled off the drag of death and the falling visions. Now he was stripped of fear, strong, night-muscled. Over the housetops he ran towards the moon. There the moon came, in a colder glory than before, attended by stars, drawing the tides of the sea. By a parapet he watched her, finding a word for each stage of her journey in the directed sky, calling her same-faced, wondering at her many masks. Death mask and dance mask over her mountainous features transformed the sky; she struggled behind a cloud, and came with a new smile over the wall of wind. Image, and all was image, from Marlais, ragged in the wind, to the appalling town, he on the roofs invisible to the street, the street beneath him blind to his walking word. His hand before him was five-fingered life.

A baby cried, but the cry grew fainter. It is all one, the loud voice and the still voice striking a common silence, the dowdy lady flattening her nose against the panes, and the well-mourned lady. The word is too much with us, and the dead word. Cloud, the last muslin's rhyme, shapes above tenements and bursts in cold rain on the suburban drives. Hail falls on cinder track and the angelled stone. It is all one, the rain and the macadam; it is all one, the hail and cinder, the flesh and the rough dust. High above the hum of the houses, far from the skyland and the frozen fence, he questioned each shadow; man among ghosts, and ghost in clover, he moved for the last answer.

The bare boy's voice through a stone mouth, no longer smoking at this hour, rose up unanswerably: 'Who walks, mad among us, on the roofs, by my cold, brick-red side and the weathercock-frozen women, walks over This street, under the image of the Welsh summer heavens walks all night loverless, has two sister lovers ten towns away. Past the great stack forests to the left and the sea his lovers burn for him endlessly by a hundred orchards.' The gossips' voices rose up unanswerably: 'Who walks by the stone

virgins is our virgin Marlais, wind and fire, and the coward
on the burning roofs.'

He stepped through the open window.

Red sap in the trees bubbled from the cauldron roots to
the last spray of blossom, and the boughs, that night after
the hollow walk, fell like candles from the trunks but could
not die for the heat of the sulphurous head of the grass
burned yellow by the dead sun. And flying there, he
rounded, half mist, half man, all apple circles on the sea-
village road in the high heat of noon as the dawn broke;
and as the sun rose like a river over the hills so the sun sank
behind a tree. The woman pointed to the hundred
orchards and the black birds who flocked around her sister,
but a wind put the trees out and he woke again. This was
the intolerable, second waking out of a life too beautiful to
break, but the dream was broken. Who had walked by the
virgins near the orchards was a virgin, wind and fire, and a
coward in the destroying coming of the morning. But after
he had dressed and taken breakfast, he walked up This street
to the hilltop and turned his face towards the invisible sea.

'Good morning, Marlais,' said an old man sitting with
six greyhounds in the blackened grass.

'Good morning, Mr David Davies.'

'You are up very early,' said David Two Times.

'I am walking towards the sea.'

'The wine-coloured sea,' said Dai Twice.

Marlais strode over the hill to the greener left, and down
behind the circle of the town to the rim of Whippet valley
where the trees, for ever twisted between smoke and slag,
tore at the sky and the black ground. The dead boughs
prayed that the roots might shoulder up the soil, leaving a
dozen channels empty for the leaves and the spirit of the
cracking wood, a hole in the valley for the mole-handed
sap, a long grave for the last spring's skeleton that once had

leapt, when the blunt and forked hills were sharp and straight, through the once-green land. But Whippet's trees were the long dead of the stacked south of the country; who had vanished under the hacked land pointed, thumb-to-hill, these black leaf-nailed and warning fingers. Death in Wales had twisted the Welsh dead into those valley cripples.

The day was a passing of days. High noon, the story-killer and the fire bug (the legends of the Russian seas died as the trees awoke to their burning), passed in all the high noons since the fall of man from the sun and the first sun's pinnacling of the half-made heavens. And all the valley summers, the once monumental red and the now headstone-featured, all that midsummer afternoon were glistening in the seaward walk. Through the ancestral valley where his fathers, out of their wooden dust and full of sparrows, wagged at a hill, he walked steadily; on the brink of the hole that held LlanAsia as a grave holds a town, he was caught in the smoke of the forests and, like a ghost from the clear-cut quarters under the stack roots, climbed down on to the climbing streets.

'Where are you walking, Marlais?' said a one-legged man by a black flower-bed.

'Towards the sea, Mr William Williams.'

'The mermaid-crowded sea,' said Will Peg.

Marlais passed out of the tubercular valley on to a waste mountain, through a seedy wood to a shagged field; a crow, on a molehill, in Prince Price's skull cawed of the breadth of hell in the packed globe; the afternoon broke down, the stumped land heaving, and, like a tree or lightning, a wind, roots up, forked between smoke and slag as the dusk dropped; surrounded by echoes, the red-hot travellers of voices, and the devils from the horned acres, he shuddered on his enemies' territory as a new night came on in the nightmare of an evening. 'Let the trees collapse,' the dusty

journeymen said, 'the boulders flake away and the gorse rot
and vanish, earth and grass be swallowed down on to a hill's
v balancing on the grave that proceeds to Eden.   Winds
on fire, through vault and coffin and fossil we'll blow a man-
full of dust into the garden.   Where the serpent sets the
tree alight, and the apple falls like a spark out of its skin, a
tree leaps up; a scarecrow shines on the cross-boughs, and,
by one in the sun, the new trees arise, making an orchard
round the crucifix.'   By midnight two more valleys lay
beneath him, dark with their two towns in the palms of the
mined mountains; a valley, by one in the morning, held
Aberbabel in its fist beneath him.   He was a young man no
longer but a legendary walker, a folk-man walking, with a
cricket for a heart; he walked by Aberbabel's chapel, cut
through the graveyard over the unstill headstones, spied a
red-cheeked man in a nightshirt two foot above ground.

The valleys passed; out of the water-dipping hills, the
moments of mountains, the eleventh valley came up like an
hour.   And coming out timelessly through the dwarf's eye
of the telescope, through the ring of light like a circle's
wedding on the last hill before the sea, the shape of the
hundred orchards magnified with the immaculate diminish-
ing of the moon.   This was the spectacle that met the
telescope, and the world Marlais saw in the morning
following upon the first of the eleven untold adventures: to
his both sides the unbroken walls, taller than the bean-
stalks that married a story on the roof of the world, of stone
and earth and beetle and tree; a graveyard before him the
ground came to a stop, shot down and down, was lost with
the devil in bed, rose shakily to the sea-village road where
the blossoms of the orchards hung over the wooden walls
and sister-roads ran off into the four white country points;
a rock line thus, straight to the hill-top, and the turning
graph scored with trees; dip down the county, deep as the

history of the final fire burning through the chamber one story over Eden, the first green structure after the red downfall; down, down, like a stone stuck with towns, like the river out of a glass of places, fell his foot-holding hill. He was a folk-man no longer but Marlais the poet walking, over the brink into ruin, up the side of doom, over hell in bed to the red left, till he reached the first of the fields where the unhatched apples were soon to cry fire in a wind from a half-mountain falling westward to the sea. A man-in-a-picture Marlais, by noon's blow to the centre, stood by a circle of apple-trees and counted the circles that travelled over the shady miles into a clump of villages. He laid himself down in the grass, and noon fell back bruised to the sun; and he slept till a handbell rang over the fields. It was a windless afternoon in the sisters' orchards, and the fair-headed sister was ringing the bell for tea.

He had come very near to the end of the indescribable journey. The fair girl, in a field sloping seaward three fields and a stile from Marlais, laid out a white cloth on a flat stone. Into one of a number of cups she poured milk and tea, and cut the bread so thin she could see London through the white pieces. She stared hard at the stile and the pruned, transparent hedge, and as Marlais climbed over, ragged and unshaven, his stripped breast burned by the sun, she rose from the grass and smiled and poured tea for him. This was the end to the untold adventures. They sat in the grass by the stone table like lovers at a picnic, too loved to speak, desireless familiars in the shade of the hedge corner. She had shaken a handbell for her sister, and called a lover over eleven valleys to her side. Her many lovers' cups were empty on the flat stone.

And he who had dreamed that a hundred orchards had broken into flame saw suddenly then in the windless after-noon tongues of fire shoot through the blossom. The trees all around them kindled and crackled in the sun, the birds flew up as a small red cloud grew from each branch, the bark caught like gorse, the unborn, blazing apples whirled down devoured in a flash. The trees were fireworks and torches, smouldered out of the furnace of the fields into a burning arc, cast down their branded fruit like cinders on the charred roads and fields.

Who had dreamed a boy's dream of her flesh-and-ghost hand in the windless afternoon saw then, at the red height, when the wooden step-roots splintered at the orchard entrance and the armed towers came to grief, that she raised her hand heavily and pointed to the trees and birds. There was a flurry in the sky, of wing and fire and near-to-evening wind in the going below of the burned day. As the new night was built, she smiled as she had done in the short dream eleven valleys old; lame like Pisa, the night leaned on the west walls; no trumpet shall knock the Welsh walls down before the last crack of music; she pointed to her sister in a shadow by the disappearing garden, and the dark-headed figure with crows on her shoulders appeared at Marlais's side.

This was the end of a story more terrible than the stories of the quick and the undead in mountainous houses on Jarvis hills, and the unnatural valley that Idris waters is a children's territory to this eleventh valley in the seaward travel. A dream that was no dream skulked there; the real world's wind came up to kill the fires; a scarecrow pointed to the extinguished trees.

This he had dreamed before the blossom's burning and the putting-out, before the rising and the salt swinging-in, was a dream no longer near these orchards. He kissed the two secret sisters, and a scarecrow kissed him back. He heard the birds fly down on to his lovers' shoulders. He saw the fork-tree breast, the barbed eye, and the dry, twig hand.

In the Direction of the Beginning

In the light tent in the swinging field in the great spring evening, near the sea and the shingled boat with a mast of cedar-wood, the hinderwood decked with beaks and shells, a folded, salmon sail, and two finned oars; with gulls in one flight high over, stork, pelican, and sparrow, flying to the ocean's end and the first grain of a timeless land that spins on the head of a sand glass, a hoop of feathers down the dark of the spring in a topsyturvy year; as the rocks in history, by every feature and scrawled limb, eye of a needle, shadow of a nerve, cut in the heart, by rifted fibre and clay thread, recorded for the rant of odyssey the dropping of the bay-leaf toppling of the oak-tree splintering of the moonstone against assassin avatar undead and numbered waves, a man was born in the direction of the beginning. And out of sleep, where the moon had raised him through the mountains in her eyes and by the strong, eyed arms that fall behind her, full of tides and fingers, to the blown sea, he wrestled over the edge of the evening, took to the beginning as a goose to the sky, and called his furies by their names from the wind-drawn index of the grave and waters. Who was this stranger who came like a hailstone, cut in ice, a snow-leafed seabush for her hair, and taller than a cedarmast, the north white rain descending and the whale-driven sea cast up to the caves of the eye, from a fishermen's city on the floating island? She was salt and white and travelling as the field, on one blade, swung with its birds around her, evening centred in the neverstill heart, he heard her hands among the treetops—a feather dived, her fingers flowed over the voices—and the world went drowning down through a siren stranger's vision of grass and waterbeasts and snow.   The world was sucked to the last lake's drop; the cataract of the last particle worried in a lather to the ground, as if the rain from heaven had let its clouds fall turtle-turning like a manna made of the soft-bellied seasons, and the hard hail, falling, spread and flustered in a cloud half flower half ash or the comb-footed scavenger's wind through a pyramid raised high with mud or the soft slow drift of mingling steam and leaves.   In the exact centre of enchantment he was a shore-man in deep sea, lashed by his hair to the eye in the cyclop breast, with his swept thighs strung among her voice; white bears swam and sailors drowned to the music she scaled and drew with hands and fables from his upright hair; she plucked his terror by the ears, and bore him singing into light through the forest of the serpent-haired and the stone-turning voice.   Revelation stared back over its transfixed shoulder.   Which was her genesis, the last spark of judgment or the first whale's spout from the waterland?   The conflagration at the end, a burial fire jumping, a spent rocket hot on its tail, or, where the first spring and its folly climbed the sea barriers and the garden locks were bruised, capped and douting water over the mountain candlehead?   Whose was the image in the wind, the print on the cliff, the echo knocking to be answered?   She was orioled and serpent-haired.   She moved in the swallowing, salty field, the chronicle and the rocks, the dark anatomies, the anchored sea itself.   She raged in the mule's womb.   She faltered in the galloping dynasty.   She was loud in the old grave, kept a still, quick tongue in the sun.   He marked her outcast image, mapped with a nightmare's foot in poison and framed against the wind, print of her thumb that buckled on its hand with a webbed shadow, interrogation of the familiar echo: which is my genesis, the granite fountain extinguishing where the first flame is cast in the sculptured world, or the bonfire maned like a lion in the threshold of the last vault? One voice then in that evening travelled the light and water waves, one lineament took on the sliding moods, from where the gold green sea cantharis dyes the trail of the octopus one venom crawled through foam, and from the four map corners one cherub in an island shape puffed the clouds to sea.

PART II

Conversation about Christmas

Small Boy. Years and years and years ago, when you were a boy——

Self. When there were wolves in Wales, and birds the colour of red-flannel petticoats whisked past the harp-shaped hills, when we sang and wallowed all night and day in caves that smelt like Sunday afternoons in damp front farmhouse parlours, and chased, with the jawbones of deacons, the English and the bears——

Small Boy. You are not so old as Mr Beynon Number Twenty-Two who can remember when there were no motors. Years and years ago, when you were a boy——

Self. Oh, before the motor even, before the wheel, before the duchess-faced horse, when we rode the daft and happy hills bare-back——

Small Boy. You're not so daft as Mrs Griffiths up the street, who says she puts her ear under the water in the reservoir and listens to the fish talk Welsh. When you were a boy, what was Christmas like?

Self. It snowed.

Small Boy. It snowed last year, too. I made a snowman and my brother knocked it down and I knocked my brother down and then we had tea.

Self. But that was not the same snow. Our snow was not only shaken in whitewash buckets down the sky, I think it came shawling out of the ground and swam and drifted out of the arms and hands and bodies of the trees; snow grew overnight on the roofs of the houses like a pure and grandfather moss, minutely ivied the walls, and settled on the postman, opening the gate, like a dumb, numb thunderstorm of white torn Christmas cards.

Small Boy. Were there postmen, then, too?

Self. With sprinkling eyes and wind-cherried noses, on spread, frozen feet they crunched up to the doors and mittened on them manfully. But all that the children could hear was a ringing of bells.

Small Boy. You mean that the postman went rat-a-tat-tat and the doors rang?

Self. The bells that the children could hear were inside them.

Small Boy. I only hear thunder sometimes, never bells.

Self. There were church bells, too.

Small Boy. Inside them?

Self. No, no, no, in the bat-black, snow-white belfries, tugged by bishops and storks. And they rang their tidings over the bandaged town, over the frozen foam of the powder and ice-cream hills, over the crackling sea. It seemed that all the churches boomed, for joy, under my window; and the weather-cocks crew for Christmas, on our fence.

Small Boy. Get back to the postmen.

Self. They were just ordinary postmen, fond of walking, and dogs, and Christmas, and the snow. They knocked on the doors with blue knuckles——

Small Boy. Ours has got a black knocker——

Self. And then they stood on the white welcome mat in the little, drifted porches, and clapped their hands together, and huffed and puffed, making ghosts with their breath, and jogged from foot to foot like small boys wanting to go out.

Small Boy. And then the Presents?

Self. And then the Presents, after the Christmas box. And the cold postman, with a rose on his button-nose, tingled down the teatray-slithered run of the chilly glinting hill.   He went in his ice-bound boots like a man on fish-monger's slabs.   He wagged his bag like a frozen camel's hump, dizzily turned the corner on one foot, and, by God, he was gone.

Small Boy. Get back to the Presents.

Self. There were the Useful Presents: engulfing mufflers of the old coach days, and mittens made for giant sloths; zebra scarves of a substance like silky gum that could be tug-o'-warred down to the goloshes; blinding tam-o'-shanters like patchwork tea-cosies, and bunnyscutted busbies and balaclavas for victims of head-shrinking tribes; from aunts who always wore wool-next-to-the-skin, there were moustached and rasping vests that made you wonder why the aunties had any skin left at all; and once I had a little crocheted nose-bag from an aunt now, alas, no longer whinnying with us.   And pictureless books in which small boys, though warned, with quotations, not to, *would* skate on Farmer Garge's pond, and did, and drowned; and books that told me everything about the wasp, except why.

Small Boy. Get on to the Useless Presents.

Self. On Christmas Eve I hung at the foot of my bed Bessie Bunter's black stocking, and always, I said, I would stay awake all the moonlit, snowlit night to hear the roof-alighting reindeer and see the hollied boot descend through soot.   But soon the sand of the snow drifted into my eyes, and, though I stared towards the fire-place and around the flickering room where the black sack-like stocking hung, I was asleep before the chimney trembled and the room was red and white with Christmas.   But in the morning, though no snow melted on the bedroom floor, the stocking bulged and brimmed: press it, it squeaked like a mouse-in-a-box; it smelt of tangerine; a furry arm lolled over, like the arm of a kangaroo out of its mother's belly; squeeze it hard in the middle, and something squelched; squeeze it again—squelch again.   Look out of the frost-scribbled window: on the great loneliness of the small hill, a blackbird was silent in the snow.

Small Boy. Were there any sweets?

Self. Of course there were sweets.   It was the marsh-mallows that squelched.   Hardboileds, toffee, fudge and allsorts, crunches, cracknels, humbugs, glaciers, and marzi-pan and butterwelsh for the Welsh.   And troops of bright tin soldiers who, if they would not fight, could always run. And Snakes-and-Families and Happy Ladders.   And Easy Hobbi-Games for Little Engineers, complete with Instruc-tions.   Oh, easy for Leonardo!   And a whistle to make the dogs bark to wake up the old man next door to make him beat on the wall with his stick to shake our picture off the wall.   And a packet of cigarettes: you put one in your mouth and you stood at the corner of the street and you waited for hours, in vain, for an old lady to scold you for smoking a cigarette and then, with a smirk, you ate it. And, last of all, in the toe of the stocking, sixpence like a silver corn.   And then downstairs for breakfast under the balloons!

Small Boy. Were there Uncles, like in our house?

Self. There are always Uncles at Christmas.   The same Uncles.   And on Christmas mornings, with dog-disturbing whistle and sugar fags, I would scour the swathed town for the news of the little world, and find always a dead bird by the white Bank or by the deserted swings: perhaps a robin, all but one of his fires out, and that fire still burning on his breast.   Men and women wading and scooping back from church or chapel, with taproom noses and wind-smacked cheeks, all albinos, huddled their stiff black jarring feathers against the irreligious snow.   Mistletoe hung from the gas in all the front parlours; there was sherry and walnuts and bottled beer and crackers by the dessert-spoons; and cats in their fur-abouts watched the fires; and the high-heaped fires crackled and spat, all ready for the chestnuts and the mulling pokers. Some few large men sat in the front parlours, without their collars, Uncles almost certainly, trying their new cigars, holding them out judiciously at arm's-length, returning them to their mouths, coughing, then holding them out again as though waiting for the explosion; and some few small aunts, not wanted in the kitchen, nor any-where else for that matter, sat on the very edges of their chairs, poised and brittle, afraid to break, like faded cups and saucers. Not many those mornings trod the piling streets: an old man always, fawn-bowlered, yellow-gloved, and, at this time of year, with spats of snow, would take his constitutional to the white bowling-green, and back, as he would take it wet or fine on Christmas Day or Doomsday; sometimes two hale young men, with big pipes blazing, no overcoats, and windblown scarves, would trudge, un-speaking, down to the forlorn sea, to work up an appetite, to blow away the fumes, who knows, to walk into the waves until nothing of them was left but the two curling smoke clouds of their inextinguishable briars.

Small Boy. Why didn't you go home for Christmas dinner?

Self. Oh, but I did, I always did. I would be slap-dashing home, the gravy smell of the dinners of others, the bird smell, the brandy, the pudding and mince, weaving up my nostrils, when out of a snow-clogged side-lane would come a boy the spit of myself, with a pink-tipped cigarette and the violet past of a black eye, cocky as a bullfinch, leering all to himself. I hated him on sight and sound, and would be about to put my dog-whistle to my lips and blow him off the face of Christmas when suddenly he, with a violet wink, put *his* whistle to *his* lips and blew so stridently, so high, so exquisitely loud, that gobbling faces, their

cheeks bulged with goose, would press against their tin-
selled windows, the whole length of the white echoing
street.

Small Boy. What did you have for Dinner?

Self. Turkey, and blazing pudding.

Small Boy. Was it nice?

Self. It was not made on earth.

Small Boy. What did you do after dinner?

Self. The Uncles sat in front of the fire, took off their
collars, loosened all buttons, put their large moist hands
over their watch-chains, groaned a little, and slept.
Mothers, aunts, and sisters scuttled to and fro, bearing
tureens. The dog was sick. Auntie Beattie had to have
three aspirins, but Auntie Hannah, who liked port, stood
in the middle of the snowbound back-yard, singing like a
big-bosomed thrush. I would blow up balloons to see how
big they would blow up to; and, when they burst, which
they all did, the Uncles jumped and rumbled. In the rich
and heavy afternoon, the Uncles breathing like dolphins
and the snow descending, I would sit in the front room,
among festoons and Chinese lanterns, and nibble at dates,
and try to make a model man-o'-war, following the Instruc-
tions for Little Engineers, and produce what might be
mistaken for a sea-going tram. And then, at Christmas
tea, the recovered Uncles would be jolly over their mince-
pies; and the great iced cake loomed in the centre of the
table like a marble grave. Auntie Hannah laced her tea
with rum, because it was only once a year. And in the
evening, there was Music. An uncle played the fiddle, a
cousin sang 'Cherry Ripe,' and another uncle sang 'Drake's
Drum.' It was very warm in the little house. Auntie
Hannah, who had got on to the parsnip wine, sang a song
about Rejected Love, and Bleeding Hearts, and Death, and
then another in which she said that her Heart was like a

Bird's Nest; and then everybody laughed again, and then I went to bed. Looking through my bedroom window, out into the moonlight and the flying, unending, smoke-coloured snow, I could see the lights in the windows of all the other houses on our hill, and hear the music rising from them up the long, steadily falling night. I turned the gas down, I got into bed. I said some words to the close and holy darkness, and then I slept.

Small Boy. But it all sounds like an ordinary Christmas.

Self. It was.

Small Boy. But Christmas when you were a boy wasn't any different to Christmas now.

Self. It was, it was.

Small Boy. Why was Christmas different then?

Self. I mustn't tell you.

Small Boy. Why mustn't you tell me? Why is Christmas different for me?

Self. I mustn't tell you.

Small Boy. Why can't Christmas be the same for me as it was for you when you were a boy?

Self. I mustn't tell you. I mustn't tell you because it is Christmas now.

How to be a Poet

An Editor, in a moment of over-confidence, has invited me to talk about this subject.

Imagine all other subjects he might have suggested: The Development of the Seduction Scene in Watts-Dunton; Charles Morgan, my favourite character in fiction; Mr T. S. Eliot and the Dollar Crisis; The Influence of Laurel and Hardy and Laurel on Hardy. As Fowler, of English Usage puts it: 'What words could not one use were those subjects but to be dealt with and referred to.' But, like a contrary cobbler, I must stick to my first.

Let me, at once, make it clear that I am not considering, in the supposedly informative jottings, Poetry as an Art or Craft, as the rhythmic verbal expression of a spiritual necessity or urge, but solely as the means to a social end; that end being the achievement of a status in society solid enough to warrant the poet discarding and expunging those affectations, so essential in the early stages, of speech, dress, and behaviour; an income large enough to satisfy his physical demands, unless he has already fallen victim to the Poet's Evil, or Great Wen; and a permanent security from the fear of having to write any more. I do not intend to ask, let alone to answer, the question: 'Is Poetry a Good Thing?' but only: 'Can Poetry be made Good Business?'

I shall, to begin with, introduce to you, with such comments as may or may not be necessary, a few of the main types of poets who have made the social and financial grade.

First, though not in order of importance, is the poet who has emerged docketed 'lyrical,' from the Civil Service.

He can be divided, so far as his physical appearance goes, into two types. He is either thin, not to say of a shagged-out appearance, with lips as fulsome, sensual, and inviting as a hen's ovipositor, bald from all too masculate birth, his eyes made small and reddened by reading books in French, a language he cannot understand, in an attic in the provinces while young and repellent, his voice like the noise of a mouse's nail on tinfoil, his nostrils transparent, his breath grey; or else he is jowled and bushy, with curved pipe and his nose full of dottle, the look of all Sussex in his stingo'd eyes, his burry tweeds smelling of the dogs he loathes, with a voice like a literate Airedale's that has learnt its vowels by correspondence course, and an intimate friend of Chesterton's, whom he never met.

Let us see in what manner our man has arrived at his present and enviable position as the Poet who has made Poetry Pay.

Dropped into the Civil Service at an age when many of our young poets now are running away to Broadcasting House, to-day's equivalent of the Sea, he is at first lost to sight in the mountains of red tape which, in future years, he is so mordantly, though with a wry and puckered smile, to dismiss in a paragraph in his 'Around and About My Shelves.' After a few years, he begins to peer out from the forms and files in which he leads his ordered, nibbling life, and picks up a cheese crumb here, a dropping there, in his ink-stained thumbs. His ears are uncannily sensitive: he can hear an opening being opened a block of offices away. And soon he learns that a poem in a Civil Service magazine is, if not a step up the ladder, at least a lick in the right direction. And he writes a poem. It is, of course, about Nature; it confesses a wish to escape from humdrum routine and embrace the unsophisticated life of the farm labourer; he desires, though

without scandal, to wake up with the birds; he expresses
the opinion that a ploughshare, not a pen, best fits his little
strength; a decorous pantheist, he is one with the rill, the
rhyming mill, the rosy-bottomed milkmaid, the russet-
cheeked rat-catcher, swains, swine, pipits, pippins. You
can smell the country in his poems, the fields, the flowers,
the armpits of Triptolemus, the barns, the pyres, the hay,
and, most of all, the corn. The poem is published. A
single lyrical extract from the beginning must suffice:

> The roaring street is hushed!
> Hushed, do I say?
> The wing of a bird has brushed
> Time's cobwebs away.
> Still, still as death, the air
> over the grey stones!
> And over the grey thoroughfare
> I hear—sweet tones!
> A blackbird open its bill,
> —A blackbird, aye!—
> And sing its liquid fill
> From the London sky.

A little time after the publication of the poem, he is nodded
to in the corridor by Hotchkiss of Inland Revenue, himself a
week-ending poet with two slim volumes to his credit, half
an inch in the Poet's Who's Who or the Newbolt Calendar,
an ambitious wife with a vee-neck and a fringe who lost the
battle of the Slade, a small car that always drives, as though
by itself, to Sussex—as a parson's horse would once unthink-
ingly trot to the public house—and an unfinished mono-
graph on the influence of Blunden on the hedgerow.

Hotchkiss, lunching with Sowerby of Customs, himself a
literary figure of importance with a weekly column in *Will
o' Lincoln's Weekly* and his name on the editorial list of the
Masterpiece of the Fortnight Club (volumes at reduced

rates to all writers, and a complete set of the works of Mary
Webb quarter-price at Christmas), says casually: 'You've
rather a promising fellow in your department, Sowerby.
Young Cribbe. I've been reading a little thing of his, "I
desire the Curlew."' And Cribbe's name goes the small,
foetid rounds.

He is next asked to contribute a *group* of poems to Hotchkiss's anthology, 'New Pipes,' which Sowerby praises—'A
rare gift for the haunting phrase'—in *Will o' Lincoln's*.
Cribbe sends copies of the anthology, each laboriously
signed: 'To the greatest living English poet, in homage,'
to twenty of the dullest poets still on their hind legs. Some
of his inscribed gifts are acknowledged. Sir Tom Knight
spares a few generous, though bemused, moments to
scribble a message on a sheet of crested writing-paper
removed, during a never-to-be-repeated week-end visit,
from a short-sighted, but not all that short-sighted peer.
'Dear Mr Crabbe,' Sir Tom writes, 'I appreciate your little
tribute. Your poem, "Nocturne with Lilies," is worthy
of Shanks. Go on. Go on. There is room on the
mount.' The fact that Cribbe's poem is not 'Nocturne
with Lilies' at all, but 'On Hearing Delius by a Lych-Gate,'
does not perturb Cribbe, who carefully files the letter, after
blowing away the dandruff, and soon is in the throes of
collecting his poems together to make, *misericordia*, a book,
'Linnet and Spindle,' dedicated 'to Clem Sowerby, that
green-fingered gardener in the Gardens of the Hesperides.'

The book appears. Some favourable notice is taken,
particularly in Middlesex. And Sowerby, too modest to
review it himself after such a gratifying dedication, reviews
it under a different name. 'This young poet,' he writes,
'is not, thanks be it, too "modernistic" to pay reverence to
the shining source of his inspiration. Cribbe will go far.'

And Cribbe goes to his publishers.   A contract is drawn
up, Messrs Stitch & Time undertake to publish his next book
of verse on condition that they have the option on his next
nine novels.   He contrives also to be engaged as a casual
reader of manuscripts to Messrs Stitch & Time, and returns
home clutching a parcel which contains a book on the
Development of the Oxford Movement in Finland by a Cotswold
Major, three blank-verse tragedies about Mary Queen of
Scots, and a novel entitled *To-morrow, Jennifer*.

Now Cribbe, until his contract, has never thought of
writing a novel.   But undaunted by the fact that he cannot tell one person from another—people, to him, are all
one dull, grey mass, except celebrities and departmental
superiors—that he has no interest whatsoever in anything
they do or say, except in so far as it concerns his career, and
that his inventive resources are as limited as those of a chip-
munk on a treadmill, he sits down in his shirt-sleeves,
loosens his collar, thumbs in the shag, and begins to study in
earnest how best, with no qualifications, to make a success
of commercial fiction.   He soon comes to the conclusion
that only quick sales and ephemeral reputations are made by
tough novels with such titles as *I've Got It Coming* or *Ten
Cents a Dice*; by proletarian novels about the conversion to
dialectical materialism of Palais-de wide boys, entitled,
maybe, *Red Rain on You, Alf*; by novels called maybe, *Melody
in Clover*, about dark men with slight limps, called Dirk
Conway and their love for two women, lascivious Ursula
Mountclare and little, shy Fay Waters.   And he soon sees
that only the smallest sales, and notices only in the loftiest
monthlies of the most limited circulation, will ever result
from his writing such a novel as *The Inner Zodiac*, by G. H. Q.
Bidet, a ruthless analysis of the idealogical conflicts arising
from the relationship between Philip Armour, an international impotent physicist, Tristram Wolf, a bisexual

sculptor in teak, and Philip's virginal but dynamic Creole wife, Titania, a lecturer in Balkan Economics, and how these highly sensitized characters—so redolent, as they are, of the post-Sartre Age—react a profound synthesis while working together, for the sake of One-ness, in a Unesco Clinic.

No fool, Cribbe realizes, even in the early stages of exploration, with theodolite and respirator through darkest Foyle, that the novel to write is that which commands a steady, unsensational, provincial, and suburban sale and concerns, for choice, the birth, education, financial ups-and-downs, marriages, separations, and deaths of five generations of a family of Lancashire cotton-brokers. This novel, he grasps at once, should be in the form of a trilogy, and each volume should bear some such solid, uneventful title as *The Warp*, *The Woof*, and *The Way*. And he sets to work. From the reviews of Cribbe's first novel, one may select: 'Here is sound craftsmanship allied to sterling characterization.' 'Incidents a-plenty.' 'You become as familiar with George Steadiman, his wife Muriel, old Tobias Matlock (a delightful vignette) and all the inhabitants of Loom House, as you do with your own family.' 'These dour Northcotes grow on you.' 'English as Manchester rain.' 'Mr Cribbe is a bull-terrier.' 'A story in the Phyllis Bottome class.' On the success of the novel, Cribbe joins the N.I.B. Club, delivers a paper on the Early Brett Young Country, and becomes a regular reviewer praising every other novel he receives—('The prose shimmers')—and inviting every third novelist to dine at the Servile Club, to which he has recently been elected.

When the whole of the trilogy has appeared, Cribbe rises, like scum, to the N.I.B. committee, attends all the memorial services for men of letters who are really dead for the first time in fifty years, tears up his old contract and signs another, brings out a new novel, which becomes a Book

Society choice, is offered, by Messrs Stitch & Time, a position in an 'advisory capacity,' which he accepts, leaves the Civil Service, buys a cottage in Bucks ('You wouldn't think it was only thirty miles from London, would you? Look, old man, see that crested grebe.' A starling flies by), a new secretary whom he later marries for her touch-typing. Poetry? Perhaps a sonnet in the *Sunday Times* every now and then; a little collection of verse once in a while ('My first love, you know'). But it doesn't really bother him any more, though it got him where he is. *He has made the grade!*

And now we must move to see for a moment a very different kind of poet, whom we shall call Cedric. To follow in Cedric's footsteps—(he'd love you to, and would never call a policeman unless it was that frightfully sinister sergeant you see sometimes in Mecklenburgh Square, just like an El Greco)—you must be born twilightly into the middle classes, or go to one of the correct schools—(which, of course, you must loathe, for it is essential, from the first, to be misunderstood)—and arrive at the University with your reputation already established as a coming poet and looking, if possible, something between a Guards' officer and a fashionable photographer's doxy. You may say: But how is one to arrive with one's reputation already established as 'a poet to watch'? (Poet-watching may in future become as popular as bird-watching. And it is quite reasonable to imagine the editorial offices of *The Poetaster* being bought up by the nation as a sanctuary.) But that is a question outside the scope of these all-too-rough notes, as it must be assumed that anyone wishing to take up Poetry as a career has always known how to turn the stuff out when required. And also Cedric's college tutor was his house-master's best friend. So here is Cedric, known already to

the discerning few for his sensitive poems about golden
limbs, sun-jewelled fronds, the ambrosia of the first shy kiss
in the delicate-traceried caverns of the moon (really the
school boot-cupboard), at the threshold of fame and the
world laid out before him like a row of balletomanes.

If this were the twenties, Cedric's first book of poems,
published while he was still an undergraduate, might be
called 'Asps and Lutes.' It would be nostalgic for a life
that never was. It would be world-weary. (He once saw
the world out of a train carriage window: it looked unreal.)
It would be a carefully garish mixture, a cunningly evoca-
tive pudding full of plums pulled from the Sitwells and
Sacheverell other people, a mildly cacophonous hothouse
of exotic horticultural and comic-erotic bric-à-brac, from
which I extract these typical lines:

> A cornucopia of phalluses
> Cascade on the vermilion palaces
> In arabesques and syrup rigadoons;
> Quince-breasted Circes of the zenanas
> Do catch this rain of cherry-wigged bananas
> And saraband beneath the raspberry moons.

After a tiff with the University authorities he vanished
into the Key of Blue—a made man.

If it were in the thirties, the title of his book might well
be *Pharos, I warn*, and would consist of one of two kinds of
verse. Either it would be made of long, lax, lackadaisical
rhythms, dying falls, and images of social awareness:

After the incessant means-test of the conspiratorial winter
Scrutinizing the tragic history of each robbed branch,
Look! the triumphant bourgeoning! spring gay as a workers'
    procession
To the newly-opened gymnasium!
Look! the full employment of the blossoms!

Or it would be daringly full of slang and street phrases, snippets of song hits, Kipling jingles, kippered blues:

We're sitting pretty
In the appalling city—
I know where we're going but I don't know where from—
Take it from me, boy,
You're my cup-of-tea, boy,
We're sitting on a big black bomb.

Social awareness! That was the motto. He would talk over coffee—('Adrian makes the best coffee in the whole of this uncivilized island.' 'Tell me, Rodney, where *do* you get these delicious pink cakes?' 'It's a secret!' 'Oh, *do* tell. And I'll give you that special receipt that Basil's Colonel brought back from Ceylon, it takes three pounds of butter and a mango pod')—of spending the long vacation in 'somewhere *really* alive. I mean, but really. Like the Rhondda Valley or something. I mean, I know I'll feel really *orientated* there. I mean, one's so stagnant here. Books, books. It's people that count. I mean, one's got to know the miners.' And he spends the long vacation with Reggie, in Bonn. A volume of politico-travel chat follows, the promise of which is amply fulfilled when, years later, he turns up as Literary Secretary of I.A.C.T. (International Arts Council To-morrow).

If Cedric were writing in the forties, he would, perhaps, be engulfed, so that he could not see the wool for the Treece, in a kind of 'apocalyptic' batter, and his first Volume might be entitled *Plangent Macrocosm*, or *Heliogabalus in Pentecost*. Cedric can mix his metaphor, bog his cliché, and soak his stolen symbols in stale ass's milk as glibly and glueily as the best of them.

Next, London and the reviewing. Reviewing, obviously,

the work of other poets. This, to do badly, is simple; and, though not at once, financially rewarding. The vocabulary that a conscientiously dishonest reviewer of contemporary verse must learn is limited. Trend, of course, and impact, impasto, awareness, *zeitgeist*, sphere of influence, Auden-esque, the latter Yeats, period of transition, constructivism, schematic, ingeniously sprinkled, will help along, no end, the short and sweeping dismissal of the life-work of any adult and responsible poet. The principal rules are few to remember: when reviewing, say, two entirely dis-similar books of verse, pit one against the other as though they were originally written in a strict competition. 'After Mr A's subtle, taut, and integrated poetical comments or near-epigrams, Mr B's long and sonorous heroic narrative, for all its textural richness and vibrative orchestration, rings curiously hollow' is an example of this most worth-while and labour-saving device. Decide, quite carefully, to be a staunch admirer of one particular poet, whether you like his poetry or not; cash in on him; make him your own; patent him; carve a niche with him. Bring his name, gratuitously, into your reviews: 'Mr E is, unfortunately, a poet much given to rhodomontade (unlike Hector Whistle).' 'Reading Mr D's admirable scholarly though, in places, pedestrian translations, we find ourselves longing for the cool ardour and consummate craftsmanship of Hector Whistle.' Be careful when you choose your poet, not to poach. Ask yourself first: 'Is Hector Whistle any-one else's pigeon?'

Read all other reviews of the books you are about to review before you say a word yourself. Quote from the poems only when pressed for time; a review should be about the reviewer, not the poet. Be careful not to slate a bad rich poet unless he is notoriously mean, dead, or in America, for it is not such a long step from reviewing verse to editing a magazine, and the rich bad poet may well put up the money.

Returning to Cedric, let us suppose that he has, as a result of comparing a rich young man's verse with Auden's to the detriment of Auden's, been given the editorship of a new literary periodical. (He may also be given a flat. If not, he should insist that the new periodical must have commodious offices. He then lives in them.) Cedric's first problem is what to call the thing. This is not easy, as most of the names that mean nothing at all—essential to the success of the new project—have all been used: *Horizon*, *Polemic*, *Harvest*, *Caravel*, *Seed*, *Transition*, *Kingdom Come*, *Focus*, *View*, *Accent*, *Apocalypse*, *Arena*, *Circus*, *Cronos*, *Signposts*, *Wind and Rain*—they've all been had. Can you hear Cedric's mind churning away? 'Vacuum,' 'Volcano,' 'Limbo,' 'Milestone,' 'Need,' 'Eruption,' 'Uterus,' 'Seismograph,' 'Vulcan,' 'Cognizance,' 'Schism,' 'Data,' 'Arson.' Yes, he's got it: 'Chiaroscuro.' And the rest is easy: just editing.

But let us look, very quickly, at some other methods of making poetry a going concern.

The Provincial Rush, or the Up-Rimbaud-and-At-'Em approach. This is not wholeheartedly to be recommended as certain qualifications are essential. Before you swoop and burst upon the centre of literary activity—which means, when you are very young, the right pubs, and, later the right flats, and later still, the right clubs—you must have behind you a body (it need have no head) of ferocious and un-understandable verse. (It is not, as I said before, my function to describe how these *gauche* and verbose ecstasies are achieved. Hart Crane found that, while listening, drunk, to Sibelius, he could turn out the stuff like billiho. A friend of mine, who has been suffering from a violent headache since he was eight, finds it so easy to write anyway, he has to tie knots in his handkerchief to remind him to stop. There are many methods, and always, when there's a will and slight delirium, there's a way.) And again, this poet must possess a thirst and constitution like that of a salt-eating pony, a hippo's hide, boundless energy, prodigious conceit, no scruples, and—most important of all, this can never be over-estimated—a home to go *back* to in the provinces whenever he breaks down.

I'm afraid I must go very rapidly through a few of the other classifications.

Of the poet who merely writes because he wants to write, who does not deeply mind if he is published or not, and who can put up with poverty and total lack of recognition in his lifetime, nothing of any pertinent value can be said. He is no business man. Posterity Does Not Pay.

Also, and highly *un*recommended, are the following:

The writing of limericks. Vast market, little or no pay.
Poems in crackers. Too seasonal.
Poems for children. This will kill you and the children.
Obituaries in verse. Only established favourites used.
Poetry as a method of blackmail (by boring). Dangerous. The one you blackmail might retaliate by reading you aloud his unfinished tragedy about St Bernard: 'The Flask.'

And lastly: *Poems on lavatory walls.* The reward is purely psychological.

Thank you.

The Followers

It was six o'clock on a winter's evening. Thin, dingy rain spat and drizzled past the lighted street lamps. The pavements shone long and yellow. In squeaking goloshes, with mackintosh collars up and bowlers and trilbies weeping, youngish men from the offices bundled home against the thistly wind—

'Night, Mr Macey.'

'Going my way, Charlie?'

'Ooh, there's a pig of a night!'

'Good night, Mr Swan.'—

and older men, clinging on to the big, black circular birds of their umbrellas, were wafted back, up the gaslit hills, to safe, hot, slippered, weatherproof hearths, and wives called Mother, and old, fond, fleabag dogs, and the wireless babbling.

Young women from the offices, who smelt of scent and powder and wet pixie hoods and hair, scuttled, giggling, arm-in-arm, after the hissing trams, and screeched as they splashed their stockings in the puddles rainbowed with oil between the slippery lines.

In a shop window, two girls undressed the dummies:

'Where you going to-night?'

'Depends on Arthur. Up she comes.'

'Mind her cami-knicks, Edna . . .'

The blinds came down over another window.

A newsboy stood in a doorway, calling the news to nobody, very softly:

'Earthquake. Earthquake in Japan.'

Water from a chute dripped on to his sacking. He waited in his own pool of rain.

A flat, long girl drifted, snivelling into her hanky, out of a jeweller's shop, and slowly pulled the steel shutters down with a hooked pole. She looked, in the grey rain, as though she were crying from top to toe.

A silent man and woman, dressed in black, carried the wreaths away from the front of their flower shop into the scented deadly darkness behind the window lights. Then the lights went out.

A man with a balloon tied to his cap pushed a shrouded barrow up a dead end.

A baby with an ancient face sat in its pram outside the wine vaults, quiet, very wet, peering cautiously all round it.

It was the saddest evening I had ever known.

A young man, with his arm round his girl, passed by me, laughing; and she laughed back, right into his handsome, nasty face. That made the evening sadder still.

I met Leslie at the corner of Crimea Street. We were both about the same age: too young and too old. Leslie carried a rolled umbrella, which he never used, though sometimes he pressed doorbells with it. He was trying to grow a moustache. I wore a check, ratting cap at a Saturday angle. We greeted each other formally:

'Good evening, old man.'

'Evening, Leslie.'

'Right on the dot, boy.'

'That's right,' I said. 'Right on the dot.'

A plump, blonde girl, smelling of wet rabbits, self-conscious even in that dirty night, minced past on high-heeled shoes. The heels clicked, the soles squelched.

Leslie whistled after her, low and admiring.

'Business first,' I said.

'Oh, boy!' Leslie said.

'And she's too fat as well.'

'I like them corpulent,' Leslie said.   'Remember Penelope Bogan? a Mrs too.'

'Oh, come *on*.   That old bird of Paradise Alley! How's the exchequer, Les?'

'One and a penny.   How you fixed?'

'Tanner.'

'What'll it be, then?   The Compasses?'

'Free cheese at the Marlborough.'

We walked towards the Marlborough, dodging umbrella spokes, smacked by our windy macs, stained by steaming lamplight, seeing the sodden, blown scourings and street-wash of the town, papers, rags, dregs, rinds, fag-ends, balls of fur, flap, float, and cringe along the gutters, hearing the sneeze and rattle of the bony trams and a ship hoot like a fog-ditched owl in the bay, and Leslie said:

'What'll we do after?'

'We'll follow someone,' I said.

'Remember following that old girl up Kitchener Street? The one who dropped her handbag?'

'You should have given it back.'

'There wasn't anything in it, only a piece of bread-and-jam.'

'Here we are,' I said.

The Marlborough saloon was cold and empty.   There were notices on the damp walls: No Singing.   No Dancing. No Gambling.   No Peddlers.

'You sing,' I said to Leslie, 'and I'll dance, then we'll have a game of nap and I'll peddle my braces.'

The barmaid, with gold hair and two gold teeth in front, like a well-off rabbit's, was blowing on her nails and polishing them on her black marocain.   She looked up as we came in, then blew on her nails again and polished them without hope.

'You can tell it isn't Saturday night,' I said. 'Evening, Miss. Two pints.'

'And a pound from the till,' Leslie said.

'Give us your one-and-a-penny, Les,' I whispered, and then said aloud: 'Anybody can tell it isn't Saturday night. Nobody sick.'

'Nobody here to *be* sick,' Leslie said.

The peeling, liver-coloured room might never have been drunk in at all. Here, commercials told jokes and had Scotches and sodas with happy, dyed, port-and-lemon women; dejected regulars grew grand and muzzy in the corners, inventing their pasts, being rich, important, and loved; reprobate grannies in dustbin black cackled and nipped; influential nobodies revised the earth; a party, with earrings, called 'Frilly Willy' played the crippled piano, which sounded like a hurdy-gurdy playing under water, until the publican's nosy wife said, 'No.' Strangers came and went, but mostly went. Men from the valleys dropped in for nine or ten; sometimes there were fights; and always there was something doing, some argie-bargie, giggle and bluster, horror or folly, affection, explosion, nonsense, peace, some wild goose flying in the boozy air of that comfortless, humdrum nowhere in the dizzy, ditchwater town at the end of the railway lines. But that evening it was the saddest room I had ever known.

Leslie said, in a low voice: 'Think she'll let us have one on tick?'

'Wait a bit, boy,' I murmured. 'Wait for her to thaw.'

But the barmaid heard me, and looked up. She looked clean through me, back through my small history to the bed I was born in, then shook her gold head.

'I don't know what it is,' said Leslie as we walked up

Crimea Street in the rain, 'but I feel kind of depressed to-night.'

'It's the saddest night in the world,' I said.

We stopped, soaked and alone, to look at the stills outside the cinema we called the Itch-pit. Week after week, for years and years, we had sat on the edges of the springless seats there, in the dank but snug, flickering dark, first with toffees and monkey-nuts that crackled for the dumb guns, and then with cigarettes: a cheap special kind that would make a fire-swallower cough up the cinders of his heart. 'Let's go in and see Lon Chaney,' I said, 'and Richard Talmadge and Milton Sills and . . . and Noah Beary,' I said, 'and Richard Dix . . . and Slim Summerville and Hoot Gibson.'

We both sighed.

'Oh, for our vanished youth,' I said.

We walked on heavily, with wilful feet, splashing the passers-by.

'Why don't you open your brolly?' I said.

'It won't open. You try.'

We both tried, and the umbrella suddenly bellied out, the spokes tore through the soaking cover; the wind danced its tatters; it wrangled above us in the wind like a ruined, mathematical bird. We tried to tug it down: an unseen, new spoke sprang through its ragged ribs. Leslie dragged it behind him, along the pavement, as though he had shot it.

A girl called Dulcie, scurrying to the Itch-pit, sniggered 'Hallo,' and we stopped her.

'A rather terrible thing has happened,' I said to her. She was so silly that, even when she was fifteen, we had told her to eat soap to make her straw hair crinkle, and Les took a piece from the bathroom, and she did.

'I know,' she said, 'you broke your gamp.'

'No, you're wrong there,' Leslie said. 'It isn't *our*

umbrella at all. It fell off the roof. *You* feel,' he said.
'You can feel it fell off the roof.' She took the umbrella
gingerly by its handle.

'There's someone up there throwing umbrellas down,' I
said. 'It may be serious.'

She began to titter, and then grew silent and anxious as
Leslie said: 'You never know. It might be walking-sticks
next.'

'Or sewing-machines,' I said.

'You wait here, Dulce, and we'll investigate,' Leslie said.

We hurried on down the street, turned a blowing corner,
and then ran.

Outside Rabiotti's café, Leslie said: 'It isn't fair on
Dulcie.' We never mentioned it again.

A wet girl brushed by. Without a word, we followed
her. She cantered, long-legged, down Inkerman Street
and through Paradise Passage, and we were at her heels.

'I wonder what's the point in following people,' Leslie
said, 'it's kind of daft. It never gets you anywhere. All
you do is follow them home and then try to look through
the window and see what they're doing and mostly
there's curtains anyway. I bet nobody else does things
like that.'

'You never know,' I said. The girl turned into St
Augustus Crescent, which was a wide lamplit mist. 'People
are always following people. What shall we call her?'

'Hermione Weatherby,' Leslie said. He was never
wrong about names. Hermione was fey and stringy, and
walked like a long gym-mistress, full of love, through the
stinging rain.

'You never know. You never know what you'll find
out. Perhaps she lives in a huge house with all her
sisters——'

'How many?'

'Seven. All full of love. And when she gets home they all change into kimonos and lie on divans with music and whisper to each other and all they're doing is waiting for somebody like us to walk in, lost, and then they'll all chatter round us like starlings and put us in kimonos too, and we'll never leave the house until we die. Perhaps it's so beautiful and soft and noisy—like a warm bath full of birds . . .'

'I don't want birds in my bath,' said Leslie. 'Perhaps she'll slit her throat if they don't draw the blinds. I don't care what happens so long as it's interesting.'

She slip-slopped round a corner into an avenue where the neat trees were sighing and the cosy windows shone.

'I don't want old feathers in the tub,' Leslie said.

Hermione turned in at number thirteen, Beach-view.

'You can see the beach all right,' Leslie said, 'if you got a periscope.'

We waited on the pavement opposite, under a bubbling lamp, as Hermione opened her door, and then we tiptoed across and down the gravel path and were at the back of the house, outside an uncurtained window.

Hermione's mother, a round, friendly, owlish woman in a pinafore, was shaking a chip-pan on the kitchen stove.

'I'm hungry,' I said.

'Ssh!'

We edged to the side of the window as Hermione came into the kitchen. She was old, nearly thirty, with a mouse-brown shingle and big earnest eyes. She wore horn-rimmed spectacles and a sensible, tweed costume, and a white shirt with a trim bow-tie. She looked as though she tried to look like a secretary in domestic films, who had only to remove her spectacles and have her hair cherished, and be dressed like a silk dog's dinner, to turn into a dazzler and make her employer Warner Baxter, gasp, woo, and marry her; but if Hermione took off her glasses, she wouldn't be able to tell if he was Warner Baxter or the man who read the meters.

We stood so near the window, we could hear the chips spitting.

'Have a nice day in the office, dear? There's weather,' Hermione's mother said, worrying the chip-pan.

'What's *her* name, Les?'

'Hetty.'

Everything there in the warm kitchen, from the tea-caddy and the grandmother clock, to the tabby that purred like a kettle, was good, dull, and sufficient.

'Mr Truscott was something awful,' Hermione said as she put on slippers.

'Where's her kimono?' Leslie said.

'Here's a nice cup of tea,' said Hetty.

'Everything's nice in that old hole,' said Leslie, grumbling. 'Where's the seven sisters like starlings?'

It began to rain much more heavily. It bucketed down on the black back yard, and the little comfy kennel of a house, and us, and the hidden, hushed town, where, even now, in the haven of the Marlborough, the submarine piano would be tinning 'Daisy,' and the happy henna'd women squealing into their port.

Hetty and Hermione had their supper. Two drowned boys watched them enviously.

'Put a drop of Worcester on the chips,' Leslie whispered; and by God she did.

'Doesn't anything happen anywhere?' I said, 'in the whole wide world? I think the *News of the World* is all made up. Nobody murders no one. There isn't any sin any more, or love, or death, or pearls and divorces and mink-coats or anything, or putting arsenic in the cocoa . . .'

'Why don't they put on some music for us,' Leslie said,

'and do a dance? It isn't every night they got two fellows watching them in the rain. Not *every* night, anyway!'

All over the dripping town, small lost people with nowhere to go and nothing to spend were gooseberrying in the rain outside wet windows, but nothing happened.

'I'm getting pneumonia,' Leslie said.

The cat and the fire were purring, grandmother time ticktocked our lives away. The supper was cleared, and Hetty and Hermione, who had not spoken for many minutes, they were so confident and close in their little lighted box, looked at one another and slowly smiled.

They stood still in the decent, purring kitchen, facing one another.

'There's something funny going to happen,' I whispered very softly.

'It's going to begin,' Leslie said.

We did not notice the sour, racing rain any more.

The smiles stayed on the faces of the two still, silent women.

'It's going to begin.'

And we heard Hetty say in a small secret voice: 'Bring out the album, dear.'

Hermione opened a cupboard and brought out a big, stiff-coloured photograph album, and put it in the middle of the table. Then she and Hetty sat down at the table, side by side, and Hermione opened the album.

'That's Uncle Eliot who died in Porthcawl, the one who had the cramp,' said Hetty.

They looked with affection at Uncle Eliot, but we could not see him.

'That's Martha-the-woolshop, you wouldn't remember her, dear, it was wool, wool, wool, with her all the time; she wanted to be buried in her jumper, the mauve one, but her husband put his foot down. He'd been in India.

That's your Uncle Morgan,' Hetty said, 'one of the Kid-welly Morgans, remember him in the snow?'

Hermione turned a page.   'And that's Myfanwy, she got queer all of a sudden, remember.   It was when she was milking.   That's your cousin Jim, the Minister, until they found out.   And that's our Beryl,' Hetty said.

But she spoke all the time like somebody repeating a lesson: a well-loved lesson she knew by heart.

We knew that she and Hermione were only waiting.

Then Hermione turned another page.   And we knew, by their secret smiles, that this was what they had been waiting for.

'My sister Katinka,' Hetty said.

'Auntie Katinka,' Hermione said.   They bent over the photograph.

'Remember that day in Aberystwyth, Katinka?' Hetty said softly.   'The day we went on the choir outing.'

'I wore my new white dress,' a new voice said.

Leslie clutched at my hand.

'And a straw hat with birds,' said the clear, new voice.

Hermione and Hetty were not moving their lips.

'I was always a one for birds on my hat.   Just the plumes of course.   It was August the third, and I was twenty-three.'

'Twenty-three come October, Katinka,' Hetty said.

'That's right, love,' the voice said.   'Scorpio I was. And we met Douglas Pugh on the Prom and he said: "You look like a queen to-day, Katinka," he said.   "You look like a queen, Katinka," he said.   Why are those two boys looking in at the window?'

We ran up the gravel drive, and around the corner of the house, and into the avenue and out on to St Augustus Crescent.   The rain roared down to drown the town. There we stopped for breath.   We did not speak or look at each other.   Then we walked on through the rain.   At Victoria corner, we stopped again.

'Good night, old man,' Leslie said.

'Good night,' I said.

And we went our different ways.

A Story

If you can call it a story. There's no real beginning or end and there's very little in the middle. It is all about a day's outing, by charabanc, to Porthcawl, which, of course, the charabanc never reached, and it happened when I was so high and much nicer.

I was staying at the time with my uncle and his wife. Although she was my aunt, I never thought of her as anything but the wife of my uncle, partly because he was so big and trumpeting and red-hairy and used to fill every inch of the hot little house like an old buffalo squeezed into an airing cupboard, and partly because she was so small and silk and quick and made no noise at all as she whisked about on padded paws, dusting the china dogs, feeding the buffalo, setting the mousetraps that never caught her; and once she sleaked out of the room, to squeak in a nook or nibble in the hayloft, you forgot she had ever been there.

But there he was, always, a steaming hulk of an uncle, his braces straining like hawsers, crammed behind the counter of the tiny shop at the front of the house, and breathing like a brass band; or guzzling and blustery in the kitchen over his gutsy supper, too big for everything except the great black boats of his boots. As he ate, the house grew smaller; he billowed out over the furniture, the loud check meadow of his waistcoat littered, as though after a picnic, with cigarette ends, peelings, cabbage stalks, birds' bones, gravy; and the forest fire of his hair crackled among the hooked hams from the ceiling. She was so small she could hit him only if she stood on a chair, and every Saturday night at half past ten he would lift her up, under his arm, on to a chair in the kitchen so that she could hit him on the head with whatever was handy, which was always a china dog. On Sundays, and when pickled, he sang high tenor, and had won many cups.

The first I heard of the annual outing was when I was sitting one evening on a bag of rice behind the counter, under one of my uncle's stomachs, reading an advertisement for sheep-dip, which was all there was to read. The shop was full of my uncle, and when Mr Benjamin Franklyn, Mr Weazley, Noah Bowen, and Will Sentry came in, I thought it would burst. It was like all being together in a drawer that smelt of cheese and turps, and twist tobacco and sweet biscuits and snuff and waistcoat. Mr Benjamin Franklyn said that he had collected enough money for the charabanc and twenty cases of pale ale and a pound apiece over that he would distribute among the members of the outing when they first stopped for refreshment, and he was about sick and tired, he said, of being followed by Will Sentry.

'All day long, wherever I go,' he said, 'he's after me like a collie with one eye. I got a shadow of my own *and* a dog. I don't need no Tom, Dick, or Harry pursuing me with his dirty muffler on.'

Will Sentry blushed, and said: 'It's only oily. I got a bicycle.'

'A man has no privacy at all,' Mr Franklyn went on. 'I tell you he sticks so close I'm afraid to go out the back in case I sit in his lap. It's a wonder to me,' he said, 'he don't follow me into bed at night.'

'Wife won't let,' Will Sentry said.

And that started Mr Franklyn off again, and they tried to soothe him down by saying: 'Don't you mind Will Sentry' . . . 'No harm in old Will' . . . 'He's only keeping an eye on the money, Benjie.'

'Aren't I honest?' asked Mr Franklyn in surprise. There was no answer for some time, then Noah Bowen said: 'You know what the committee is. Ever since Bob the Fiddle they don't feel safe with a new treasurer.'

'Do you think *I*'m going to drink the outing funds, like Bob the Fiddle did?' said Mr Franklyn.

'You *might*,' said my uncle slowly.

'I resign,' said Mr Franklyn.

'Not with our money you won't,' Will Sentry said.

'Who put dynamite in the salmon pool?' said Mr Weazley, but nobody took any notice of him. And, after a time, they all began to play cards in the thickening dusk of the hot, cheesy shop, and my uncle blew and bugled whenever he won, and Mr Weazley grumbled like a dredger, and I fell to sleep on the gravy-scented mountain meadow of uncle's waistcoat.

On Sunday evening, after Bethesda, Mr Franklyn walked into the kitchen where my uncle and I were eating sardines with spoons from the tin because it was Sunday and his wife would not let us play draughts. She was somewhere in the kitchen, too. Perhaps she was inside the grandmother clock, hanging from the weights and breathing. Then, a second later, the door opened again and Will Sentry edged into the room, twiddling his hard, round hat. He and Mr Franklyn sat down on the settee, stiff and moth-balled and black in their chapel and funeral suits.

'I brought the list,' said Mr Franklyn. 'Every member fully paid. You ask Will Sentry.'

My uncle put on his spectacles, wiped his whiskery mouth with a handkerchief big as a Union Jack, laid down his spoon of sardines, took Mr Franklyn's list of names, removed the spectacles so that he could read, and then ticked the names off one by one.

'Enoch Davies. Aye. He's good with his fists. You

never know. Little Gerwain. Very melodious bass. Mr
Cadwalladwr. That's right. He can tell opening time
better than my watch. Mr Weazley. Of course. He's
been to Paris. Pity he suffers so much in the charabanc.
Stopped us nine times last year between the Beehive and the
Red Dragon. Noah Bowen, ah, very peaceable. He's got
a tongue like a turtle-dove. Never a argument with Noah
Bowen. Jenkins Loughor. Keep him off economics. It
cost us a plate-glass window. And ten pints for the Sergeant. Mr Jervis. Very tidy.'

'He tried to put a pig in the charra,' Will Sentry said.

'Live and let live,' said my uncle.

Will Sentry blushed.

'Sinbad the Sailor's Arms. Got to keep in with him.
Old O. Jones.'

'Why old O. Jones?' said Will Sentry.

'Old O. Jones always goes,' said my uncle.

I looked down at the kitchen table. The tin of sardines
was gone. By Gee, I said to myself, Uncle's wife is quick
as a flash.

'Cuthbert Johnny Fortnight. Now there's a card,' said
my uncle.

'He whistles after women,' Will Sentry said.

'So do you,' said Mr Benjamin Franklyn, 'in your mind.'

My uncle at last approved the whole list, pausing only to
say, when he came across one name: 'If we weren't a
Christian community, we'd chuck that Bob the Fiddle in the
sea.'

'We can do that in Porthcawl,' said Mr Franklyn, and
soon after that he went, Will Sentry no more than an inch
behind him, their Sunday-bright boots squeaking on the
kitchen cobbles.

And then, suddenly, there was my uncle's wife standing
in front of the dresser, with a china dog in one hand. By

Gee, I said to myself again, did you ever see such a woman, if that's what she is. The lamps were not lit yet in the kitchen and she stood in a wood of shadows, with the plates on the dresser behind her shining—like pink-and-white eyes.

'If you go on that outing on Saturday, Mr Thomas,' she said to my uncle in her small, silk voice, 'I'm going home to my mother's.'

Holy Mo, I thought, she's got a mother. Now that's one old bald mouse of a hundred and five I won't be wanting to meet in a dark lane.

'It's me or the outing, Mr Thomas.'

I would have made my choice at once, but it was almost half a minute before my uncle said: 'Well, then, Sarah, it's the outing, my love.' He lifted her up, under his arm, on to a chair in the kitchen, and she hit him on the head with the china dog. Then he lifted her down again, and then I said good night.

For the rest of the week my uncle's wife whisked quiet and quick round the house with her darting duster, my uncle blew and bugled and swole, and I kept myself busy all the time being up to no good. And then at breakfast time on Saturday morning, the morning of the outing, I found a note on the kitchen table. It said: 'There's some eggs in the pantry. Take your boots off before you go to bed.' My uncle's wife had gone, as quick as a flash.

When my uncle saw the note, he tugged out the flag of his handkerchief and blew such a hubbub of trumpets that the plates on the dresser shook. 'It's the same every year,' he said. And then he looked at me. 'But this year it's different. *You*'ll have to come on the outing, too, and what the members will say I dare not think.'

The charabanc drew up outside, and when the members of the outing saw my uncle and me squeeze out of the shop together, both of us cat-licked and brushed in our Sunday best, they snarled like a zoo.

'Are you bringing a *boy*?' asked Mr Benjamin Franklyn as we climbed into the charabanc.   He looked at me with horror.

'Boys is nasty,' said Mr Weazley.

'He hasn't paid his contributions,' Will Sentry said.

'No room for boys.   Boys get sick in charabancs.'

'So do you, Enoch Davies,' said my uncle.

'Might as well bring *women*.'

The way they said it, women were worse than boys.

'Better than bringing grandfathers.'

'Grandfathers is nasty too,' said Mr Weazley.

'What can we do with him when we stop for refreshments?'

'I'm a grandfather,' said Mr Weazley.

'Twenty-six minutes to opening time,' shouted an old man in a panama hat, not looking at a watch.   They forgot me at once.

'Good old Mr Cadwalladwr,' they cried, and the charabanc started off down the village street.

A few cold women stood at their doorways, grimly watching us go.   A very small boy waved good-bye, and his mother boxed his ears.   It was a beautiful August morning.

We were out of the village, and over the bridge, and up the hill towards Steeplehat Wood when Mr Franklyn, with his list of names in his hand, called out loud: 'Where's old O. Jones?'

'Where's old O?'

'We've left old O behind.'

'Can't go without old O.'

And though Mr Weazley hissed all the way, we turned and drove back to the village, where, outside the Prince of

Wales, old O. Jones was waiting patiently and alone with a canvas bag.

'I didn't want to come at all,' old O. Jones said as they hoisted him into the charabanc and clapped him on the back and pushed him on a seat and stuck a bottle in his hand, 'but I always go.' And over the bridge and up the hill and under the deep green wood and along the dusty road we wove, slow cows and ducks flying by, until 'Stop the bus!' Mr Weazley cried. 'I left my teeth on the mantelpiece.'

'Never you mind,' they said, 'you're not going to bite nobody,' and they gave him a bottle with a straw.

'I might want to smile,' he said.

'Not you,' they said.

'What's the time, Mr Cadwalladwr?'

'Twelve minutes to go,' shouted back the old man in the panama, and they all began to curse him.

The charabanc pulled up outside the Mountain Sheep, a small, unhappy public-house with a thatched roof like a wig with ringworm. From a flagpole by the Gents fluttered the flag of Siam. I knew it was the flag of Siam because of cigarette cards. The landlord stood at the door to welcome us, simpering like a wolf. He was a long, lean, black-fanged man with a greased love-curl and pouncing eyes. 'What a beautiful August day!' he said, and touched his love-curl with a claw. That was the way he must have welcomed the Mountain Sheep before he ate it, I said to myself. The members rushed out, bleating, and into the bar.

'You keep an eye on the charra,' my uncle said; 'see nobody steals it now.'

'There's nobody to steal it,' I said, 'except some cows,' but my uncle was gustily blowing his bugle in the bar. I looked at the cows opposite, and they looked at me. There was nothing else for us to do. Forty-five minutes passed, like a very slow cloud. The sun shone down on the lonely road, the lost, unwanted boy, and the lake-eyed cows. In the dark bar they were so happy they were breaking glasses. A Shoni-Onion Breton man, with a beret and a necklace of onions, bicycled down the road and stopped at the door.

'Quelle un grand matin, monsieur,' I said.

'There's French, boy bach!' he said.

I followed him down the passage, and peered into the bar. I could hardly recognize the members of the outing. They had all changed colour. Beetroot, rhubarb, and puce, they hollered and rollicked in that dark, damp hole like enormouse ancient bad boys, and my uncle surged in the middle, all red whiskers and bellies. On the floor was broken glass and Mr Weazley.

'Drinks all round,' cried Bob the Fiddle, a small, absconding man with bright blue eyes and a plump smile.

'Who's been robbing the orphans?'

'Who sold his little babby to the gyppoes?'

'Trust old Bob, he'll let you down.'

'You will have your little joke,' said Bob the Fiddle, smiling like a razor, 'but I forgive you, boys.'

Out of the fug and babel I heard: 'Come out and fight.'

'No, not now, later.'

'No, now when I'm in a temper.'

'Look at Will Sentry, he's proper snobbled.'

'Look at his wilful feet.'

'Look at Mr Weazley lording it on the floor.'

Mr Weazley got up, hissing like a gander. 'That boy pushed me down deliberate,' he said, pointing to me at the door, and I slunk away down the passage and out to the mild, good cows. Time clouded over, the cows wondered, I threw a stone at them and they wandered, wondering, away. Then out blew my uncle, ballooning, and one by one the members lumbered after him in a grizzle. They had drunk the Mountain Sheep dry. Mr Weazley had won

a string of onions that the Shoni-Onion man raffled in the
bar. 'What's the good of onions if you left your teeth
on the mantelpiece?' he said. And when I looked through
the back window of the thundering charabanc, I saw
the pub grow smaller in the distance. And the flag of
Siam, from the flagpole by the Gents, fluttered now at
half mast.

The Blue Bull, the Dragon, the Star of Wales, the Twll
in the Wall, the Sour Grapes, the Shepherd's Arms, the
Bells of Aberdovey: I had nothing to do in the whole, wild
August world but remember the names where the outing
stopped and keep an eye on the charabanc. And whenever
it passed a public-house, Mr Weazley would cough like a
billygoat and cry: 'Stop the bus, I'm dying of breath!' And
back we would all have to go.

Closing time meant nothing to the members of that
outing. Behind locked doors, they hymned and rumpused
all the beautiful afternoon. And, when a policeman
entered the Druid's Tap by the back door, and found them
all choral with beer, 'Sssh!' said Noah Bowen, 'the pub is
shut.'

'Where do you come from?' he said in his buttoned,
blue voice.

They told him.

'I got a auntie there,' the policeman said. And very
soon he was singing 'Asleep in the Deep.'

Off we drove again at last, the charabanc bouncing with
tenors and flagons, and came to a river that rushed along
among willows.

'Water!' they shouted.

'Porthcawl!' sang my uncle.

'Where's the donkeys?' said Mr Weazley.

And out they lurched, to paddle and whoop in the cool,
white, winding water. Mr Franklyn, trying to polka on the

slippery stones, fell in twice. 'Nothing is simple,' he said with dignity as he oozed up the bank.

'It's cold!' they cried.

'It's lovely!'

'It's smooth as a moth's nose!'

'It's *better* than Porthcawl!'

And dusk came down warm and gentle on thirty wild, wet, pickled, splashing men without a care in the world at the end of the world in the west of Wales. And, 'Who goes there?' called Will Sentry to a wild duck flying.

They stopped at the Hermit's Nest for a rum to keep out the cold. 'I played for Aberavon in 1898,' said a stranger to Enoch Davies.

'Liar,' said Enoch Davies.

'I can show you photos,' said the stranger.

'Forged,' said Enoch Davies.

'And I'll show you my cap at home.'

'Stolen.'

'I got friends to prove it,' the stranger said in a fury.

'Bribed,' said Enoch Davies.

On the way home, through the simmering moon-splashed dark, old O. Jones began to cook his supper on a primus stove in the middle of the charabanc. Mr Weazley coughed himself blue in the smoke. 'Stop the bus,' he cried, 'I'm dying of breath!' We all climbed down into the moonlight. There was not a public-house in sight. So they carried out the remaining cases, and the primus stove, and old O. Jones himself, and took them into a field, and sat down in a circle in the field and drank and sang while old O. Jones cooked sausage and mash and the moon flew above us. And there I drifted to sleep against my uncle's mountainous waistcoat, and, as I slept, 'Who goes there?' called out Will Sentry to the flying moon.